BEAT TO A PULP

BEAT TO A PULP
HARDBOILED 3

Edited by
David Cranmer
& Elise Wright

Cover image from iStock; Design by dMix.
ISBN: 978-0-9912039-0-1

BEAT to a PULP
PO Box 173
Freeville, New York 13068
USA
Email: btapzine@beattoapulp.com
Visit us at www.beattoapulp.com

CONTENTS

One Ashore in Singapore

Andrew Nette

A postcard-sized sign beside an open doorway announced Chance had arrived at his destination, the Eastern Hemisphere Trading Co. Clearly a business that didn't rely on passing trade.

Chance wiped the sweat from his forehead. He'd stopped the taxi at the beginning of Joo Chiat Road and had walked for thirty minutes. He figured it would be easier to find the office on foot. Besides, the arctic temperature and easy listening music inside the vehicle on top of the six-hour Sydney to Singapore flight had left him in desperate need of fresh air.

The building was one in a long line of Chinese shop houses sandwiched between a karaoke lounge and an acupuncturist. A life-sized male anatomical model stood to attention in the front window of the latter. A plastic skull half stripped of flesh leered at him.

Chance entered and climbed the wooden stairs. A large Indian man in a shirt and sarong squatted on the landing. Chance stopped at a polite distance but kept his eyes fixed on the Indian.

"Is Mister Tan in?"

The man's gaze narrowed. "Please wait here, sir." He disappeared up the stairs.

He returned several moments later. "Thank you, sir, this way."

The Indian led him up the stairs to a smoked glass door and followed Chance inside, shutting the door behind them.

Chance hadn't given much thought to Jimmy Tan. If he had, he would have imagined a scrawny old Asian guy, badly dyed hair, his demeanour half patrician Chinese, half street hustler. Much like the man who'd sent him to Singapore.

Instead he stood in front of a tubby twenty-something with a pale, round face and designer glasses, who tapped away on a laptop with one hand while using chopsticks with the other to scoop noodles from a bowl. He finished slurping a noodle and glanced at Chance with an annoyed look.

"It's not ready yet," he snapped and shovelled more noodles into his mouth.

Conscious of the bodyguard behind him, Chance stood still, hands at his sides. "When will it be finished?"

"Tomorrow, maybe the day after," the young man shrugged, eyes on the screen in front of him. "It's a big job, takes time."

His Singaporean English had an American accent. Old man Tan had no doubt packed his son off to university in the States. No prizes for guessing his subject. Every inch of desk space was covered in computer equipment. More lined the shelves. Tiny lights flashed and wiring sprouted in all directions. The office looked like the set of a B-grade science fiction movie.

"Didn't you hear?" Tan looked up at Chance as if he was a particularly thick student. "What you've come for is not ready. Go to your hotel. I'll call when it's finished."

The Indian opened the door and stood to one side so Chance could exit.

* * *

The hotel was a shit-hole. A tiny room, decor stripped down to the basics, whatever couldn't be nailed down or stolen. The only thing it had going was location—in the middle of Singapore's Little India.

Chance dumped his duffle bag on the bed, flicked through the TV stations then opted for a walk.

The streets teemed with South Asians. They crowded around bars to watch the cricket or sat in restaurants eating curries off banana leaves. Most were men, migrant labourers judging from the queue in front of the Western Union office.

Chance was reminded of backpacking in his twenties before he'd joined the army. The air smelt of the incense, spices and jasmine sold from footpath stalls. The screech of a dozen Bollywood soundtracks competed for his attention.

It was a world away from the Asia-lite image of Singapore cultivated on the in-flight entertainment on the way over, shots of androgenous, vaguely Asian-looking people dressed in white, lounging around apartments or in restaurants, smug with prosperity.

Chance had no doubt his employer had picked the hotel in Little India because it was cheap. The old Chinaman would have insisted he sail to Singapore had the job not been a priority.

Dao Ming, Mister Long's daughter and protégé, had called Chance a couple of days earlier and asked him to fly to Singapore to take delivery of a package. He was to bring it straight back to the Jade Dragon, the restaurant they owned off the main drag in Yass, a smudge of a town sixty kilometres north of Australia's capital city, Canberra—the front for the old man's illegal activities.

"What's in the package?" Chance asked.

"That is of no concern to you," said Dao Ming.

It felt weird taking marching orders from a teenage girl. But while most women her age were gossiping about boys and wasting time on Facebook, Dao Ming was learning the ropes of her father's business.

"Listen princess, it's my arse on the line. Singapore has an enthusiastic capital punishment policy. If I get busted holding something I shouldn't it'll be my neck that ends up in the noose." Chance paused for dramatic effect. "Now do you want to tell me what I'm picking up or do you want to find someone else to be your courier?"

She sighed. "Documents."

"Documents? Why don't you just get them sent by registered mail?"

"My father is worried some petty thief in the post office may steal them."

"You honestly don't see the irony in that, do you?"

"You want the job or not?" she said, bored by the conversation.

As with most things in Chance's life, the association with Mister Long had occurred by accident. Chance had been part of a gang robbing a payroll from a carnival on the south coast of New South Wales. That the job had gone badly was an understatement. Chance ended up being blackmailed by bikies to locate a million dollars in lost drug money. The trail had led to the Jade Dragon Restaurant. Mister Long had given him the location of the money and cut a side deal with Chance to recover stolen narcotics.

Since then, Chance received regular phone calls from Dao Ming, never her father. She always gave him the minimum information to perform the task, mainly pick-ups and deliveries, occasionally frightening off potential competitors.

Each job had opened the door, just a crack, on Long's business operations. Chance enjoyed the view, but never wanted to see much more. He was paid well for his work and it suited him not to have to think about the details. The Singapore job looked simple. The only challenge Chance could see so far was reigning in his urge to deck Jimmy Tan.

But the frosty, condescending tone had disappeared from Tan's voice when he rang Chance's hotel room the next morning. It took Chance a few moments to recognise the caller.

"My associates are just putting the finishing touches on the goods," Tan oozed. "It shouldn't be long now."

"Appreciate the update," said Chance, about to hang up.

"There's also another matter I would like to discuss with you."

Chance said nothing.

"There's a café several doors left of my building. Meet me there in an hour."

Tan was the café's only customer when Chance arrived. He was eating a small mountain of fried rice. In his white polo shirt and shorts, he looked like a tennis umpire on a break between matches.

"Have you eaten?" Tan asked.

"Just coffee, thanks."

Tan screwed up his face, bewildered anyone would refuse an offer of food. He signalled to a woman in a hijab behind the counter.

"So, how is old man Long?" Tan asked between mouthfuls of rice.

"Fine."

"And the lovely Dao Ming? She's an ambitious woman. Her father's daughter in every sense."

"Tell me about it."

The two sat in silence as the woman put a cup of black coffee in front of Chance and returned to her position behind the counter.

"Long and my father were very good friends. They were in the same brotherhood back in the days when Singapore was not so civilised. He must trust you a great deal to take charge of such precious cargo."

Chance grunted, took a sip of his coffee, waiting for Tan to get to the point.

"But I'm guessing you don't know what you're picking up." Tan looked at Chance mischievously.

"Documents," Chance said, aware he was at a disadvantage.

"Documents is such an old-fashioned term. I prefer to think of what I do more as managing data for people who want to make a fresh start."

"You mean you forge things?"

"My father forged things." Tan shot Chance an offended look. "He was one of the best passport forgers in Singapore. I do much more than that.

"Don't get me wrong, it's still important to get the basics right. But it's also necessary to create other aspects of identity, especially if the individual concerned is likely to come under any sort of official surveillance.

"Think of it this way," he continued, seeing the frown on Chance's face.

"Most of us have a data shadow that follows us around. Every time you do an electronic bank transfer, go through airport immigration control or send an email you add to it. The absence of a data shadow is like a red flag to high-tech police and security services."

Tan laid down his chopsticks. "I don't just forge the necessary documents. I create an entirely new identity, complete with a data shadow."

Chance raised his eyebrows, impressed by Tan in spite of himself.

"It's not a hundred per cent foolproof," Tan added, "but it would take a clever cop with the right equipment and a lot of time to crack it."

"Interesting." Chance drained his coffee. "But you didn't bring me here to boast about your business."

"No. I have a proposition for how you might profitably spend your time in Singapore until your goods are ready."

Chance nodded for Tan to continue.

"In addition to creating data, I also collect it. A few weeks ago, a valuable piece of data in my possession was stolen. This item could anger some very powerful people if it got into the wrong hands, especially if it goes public."

Chance leaned forward and looked at Tan with renewed interest. "Exactly what kind of data are we talking about?"

"Data of a visual kind," replied Tan, sheepishly.

"Pictures?"

"Yes."

"Of someone doing something they shouldn't."

Tan readjusted his glasses on his nose and gave Chance a weak smile. "Yes'.

"And you want to get them back."

"The people who have this data have already been in contact with me. Negotiations have taken place, money exchanged, a time and place has been arranged. All I need is a safe pair of hands to take delivery and bring it to me."

"What about that Indian I saw at your office yesterday? He's big enough, why don't you use him?"

"Aadish? No, I want someone with no links to Singapore."

"Or to yourself," said Chance.

"Yes." Tan looked away and signalled to the woman behind the counter. "But from what I was able to find out about you, *Gary*, I think you're the right man for the job."

"What do you mean?"

"As I said, I don't just create data, I collect it. I was able to find out quite a lot about you, your time in the Australian army, your broken marriage. There a few other bits and pieces, less so over the last couple of years." Tan gave Chance a satisfied smile. "I was not able to find out, for example, how you lost the little finger on your left hand."

Chance glanced at his hand with the missing digit, the legacy of his first heist. He stared at Tan in silence, letting the Singaporean's question hang unanswered in the air. Tan was saved from further discomfort by the arrival of the woman who placed a second serving of rice in front of him.

"I'll pay you five thousand US dollars, transferred to a bank of your choice. It'll be between us. I guarantee the old man back in Australia will hear nothing of it."

Chance blew his cheeks out and leaned back in his chair. "When's the pick-up?" he said.

"Midnight tonight."

"Make it ten thousand, mate, and you've got yourself a courier."

* * *

The elevator took Chance to the penthouse of an upmarket block of apartments a stone's throw from Orchard Road, Singapore's main retail strip.

He'd arrived a couple of hours before midnight and sat in an adjacent square of parkland, watching the entrance. When the time came, he pressed the intercom button of the apartment number he'd been given by Tan and announced his purpose. There was no reply but the door clicked open, and he went inside.

The elevator door opened onto a carpeted hallway. He followed it to a large room furnished with a small bar, couches, and sculptures on pedestals. A giant fish tank against one wall bathed the room in soft blue light. On the far side of the room a set of glass double doors led to a patio with a view of the city lights.

One of the glass doors slid open and a stylish Asian woman in a black, knee-length evening dress stepped inside, a whiff of cigarette smoke following her.

Tan had told Chance the other side would also be using a go-between.

She looked him over and walked towards the bar, unscrewed the top off a bottle of Russian vodka and poured two large shots.

"So you are the *ang mo* courier Tan has sent to collect his goods," she said over her shoulder in heavily accented English.

He stood close enough to smell her perfume. His broad face, short blond hair, solid tradesman's build, were reflected along with the woman in the glass of a framed Chinese revolutionary poster above the bar. She turned, a look on her face Chance couldn't decipher, and held out a glass in a hand with long scarlet nails. Chance was about to accept the drink when he saw someone else in the reflection, an Asian man in a suit raising his hand.

Chance grabbed the woman hard by both shoulders and wheeled her around just as the knife struck, hitting her deep in the back. Her large brown eyes looked up at him in surprise, then she slumped against him. Chance let her slide to the ground, grabbed the nearest object, an expensive-looking vase, and threw it at the man. He dodged it with ease and it smashed against the wall.

The man pounced across a sofa and aimed a kick at Chance. Chance ducked, and the man landed cat-like on his feet, picked up a silver ice bucket from the bar and swung it, shards of ice scattering like broken glass. Chance felt the bucket connect hard with the side of his head, before he was hurled backwards by a kick in the ribs.

The man withdrew his knife from the prone woman and approached. Chance scrambled to his feet and snatched at a nearby floor lamp. He yanked it, pulling the plug out of the wall, and grasped the metal pole in both hands. He used it to block a knife thrust, knocked the blade out of the man's hand, and rammed the base into his assailant's stomach.

The man doubled over. Chance raised the lamp and brought the base down hard on the man's head, pounding away until his assailant stopped moving.

Chance dropped the lamp, staggered to the bar and took a long slug from the vodka bottle. He felt the side of his head, his fingers coming away bloody, and heard the woman groan.

"Hospital," she murmured as he leaned over her.

"Photos first," he lied. She didn't have long and taking her to the hospital was a risk he couldn't take.

"Desk .... Bedroom."

The pictures were easy to find, a dozen glossy A4 black and whites of a distinguished older Asian man putting the moves on three voluptuous blonde women, his face clearly visible amid white flesh.

Chance slid the pictures back into their manila envelope along with a memory card, and then tossed the rest of the bedroom. In the walk-in wardrobe he found a backpack half full of bundles of Singaporean dollars. Under a pile of silk underwear in a chest of draws were a set of handcuffs, a riding crop and a small tin of blue pills. Dragon lady clearly liked to play rough, but the game tonight had gotten out of hand.

Chance had another slug of vodka and went through his options. The situation wasn't good.

He'd just beaten one person to death and used another as a human shield.

The apartment was covered in his DNA, too much to remove.

He hadn't seen a single cop since arriving in Singapore, but he'd noticed closed-circuit TV cameras everywhere. For all he knew, there was already video of him entering the apartment.

Luckily, his passport and wallet were on him; he couldn't risk going back to his hotel. He had a plan but he needed somewhere safe to stay until morning when he could put it into action.

Chance washed the blood from the side of his head, put the manila envelope in the backpack with the money and left. Outside, he paused to get his bearings, and headed for Orchard Road.

He followed the neon trail of brand names until he came to a four-storey building. The sidewalk was bustling despite the late hour. Men arrived solo and left with company. Drivers lounged against parked taxis. A cripple in a wheelchair hawked roses. An elderly man held up a briefcase full of watches in front of him. "Time is money," he kept repeating under his breath.

Chance approached a group of woman. One peeled off, slim, with a tight, leopard-print dress and long, straight black hair.

"Hello, handsome," she cooed. "My name is Celine. You want a friend?"

Chance hooked an arm in hers and manoeuvred the woman to the nearest taxi.

"Darling, are you hurt?" She made to touch the side of his head.

"I'm okay," he said and brushed her away.

"We go to your place?" she said as they got into the taxi.

"No. Do you know somewhere else? All night. I'll pay as much as you want."

She leaned forward and spoke to the driver.

Fifteen minutes later the taxi stopped in front of a rundown hotel. The receptionist was a young guy, spiked black hair, tipped red, a T-shirt that read, "It's only illegal if you get caught."

"Amen to that, brother," muttered Chance. The receptionist didn't look up from his iPhone.

The room was a carbon copy of the one in Little India. Chance showered and sat on the bed, feeling for injuries. There was a bruise where he'd been kicked but nothing felt broken.

He stood as Celine emerged from the bathroom. She was wrapped in a towel. Let it fall. Her breasts were small, so was her cock. It was the second time tonight things hadn't gone as planned but he had nowhere else to go. She took Chance in her mouth before he could protest.

* * *

Jimmy Tan froze when he saw Chance sitting in his office wearing a baseball cap and dark glasses, his feet on the desk.

Chance smiled, put down the computer magazine he'd been reading, and pointed the Glock pistol he'd found in one of the desk drawers at Tan.

"Morning, Jimmy."

"Where's Aadish?" said Tan.

Chance gestured with the gun to a corner where the big Indian was slumped, tied up and unconscious.

"He didn't know what hit him." Chanced grimaced. "As you might already have heard, things didn't quite go as planned last night."

"I swear, what happened had nothing to do with me," Tan stammered, his face popping sweat. "I paid the money, like I told you. The pick-up should have happened without incident. It was their go-between. She was operating on her own initiative. The other side has been in contact with me, and they want you to know how sorry they are."

"Honour among thieves, is that how it is Jimmy?

"I've been so worried, I haven't even eaten this morning." Tan said. "I would never do anything to damage my relationship with Mister Long."

"Strange as it seems, Jimmy, I believe you."

Tan exhaled loudly as Chance put the gun on the desk.

"And I have your photos."

"Where are they?"

"Somewhere safe."

"I don't understand."

"Two people died last night, probably double Singapore's monthly homicide rate. Now I'm a fugitive. The pictures are my insurance. You get them once you help me get off this fucking island."

"But what can I do?" Tan whined.

"I can think of something. But it's going to have to be a rush job."

* * *

The queue at passport control moved quickly, Singaporean and foreign businesspeople, holidaying families returning home. Among the crowd was a short, dark-haired man in a stylish, lightweight grey suit, white shirt open at the neck, who constantly scanned his surroundings.

Celine had proved a useful companion. She'd done a good job changing Chance's appearance, chosen new clothes, and even found him a place to stay while Tan sorted out Chance's new identity. Money, enough to pay for the rest of her sex change surgery, had bought Celine's cooperation. Her loathing of the police had bought her silence.

The killings had been front-page news. The woman was a member of Singapore high society, married to a wealthy banker who was away in Europe on business. The knife man was a Taiwanese national. The police were clear he'd murdered her, but whoever smashed in his skull remained at large.

Chance patted his shoulder bag. In it were the photographs, the memory card, and three sets of ID: his original passport, the one he'd originally come to Singapore to collect for Mister Long, and another, prepared by Tan in the name of Phillip Green, a thirty-three-year-old English software engineer. Tan had used his contacts at Singapore immigration to fix their database to show Green arriving in Singapore three days earlier for a meeting en route to Sydney.

Chance's heartbeat quickened as he handed Green's passport to the immigration officer. She gave it a hard look, glanced at him, and put it under the scanner. She offered him a sweet from a small glass bowl on the counter while she stamped it and waved him through.

He wandered for several minutes, waiting for a hand on his shoulder. When it didn't come, he went to the bar and ordered a beer, nursed it until his flight was called.

Chance found a mailbox on the way to the departure gate, took the envelope with the photos and memory card out of his shoulder bag. He pushed it through the slot and hurried to catch his flight.

†

Doe in Headlights

Patti Abbott

After exiting the highway, turn left on the gravel road across from a yellow Cadillac.

Doe looked around—near-sightedly, of course, since she hated wearing her glasses. The question she'd been asking herself for three hours—how could Feck know that the car would definitely be parked there—was answered when she saw the sun-bleached Caddy was up on blocks. She might not have known the color if her directions hadn't said yellow. The house behind it looked as just as faded—it was hard to determine the color of the shutters or even the front door. How much time had passed since the last paint job?

She shivered and turned up the heat. November in Michigan, right. Just one-hundred and fifty miles northwest of Detroit, but she was in another climate. This area—and she could easily picture its position on the left hand everyone in Michigan used to point out a spot in the state—was a popular summer destination. But on a gray, late autumn day, there was no sign of mini-golf, T-shirt shops, or kayaks. Where *was* the lake anyway? She made the turn, map in her mouth now, and crept along looking for:

A banged-up, pre-fab boathouse.

There it was, and "banged-up" was putting a good face on it. It looked glued together—like the popsicle-stick log cabins she made as a kid in Brownies. She took the next right and the gravel gave way to dry, sandy dirt covered with pine needles and decaying leaves from the trees towering above. Hadn't this been the setting for that goofy horror movie—the one Feck tried to explain to her when they were high on something?

She'd been working for Feck for nearly two years, starting immediately after his former employee and her former friend, Ruthie, took a flyer and moved to Vegas.

"She's got the legs for it, Doe," Feck said, throwing Ruthie's scrawled note on the table. "Showgirl gams."

"She's cleaning hotel rooms," she told him. "Or toting a tray. She may have the legs, but she doesn't have the feet." Ruthie was the most graceless person she knew.

Up until that minute, Doe's name had been Delores, and it took her a minute to realize she'd been renamed.

"How do you spell that?" she asked him. "How do you spell Doe?"

He spelled it for her, and that was that. The same night, they had sex for the first time. She could still smell Ruthie on his sheets. And it wasn't perfume since Ruthie didn't wear any. *Ruthie on the Sheets*, as she thought of that scent, was soon replaced.

Doe was a waitress at a bunch of dumpy places outside Detroit before then. She supposed her job with Feck wasn't much better, but it had more variety. Feck was good at mixing things up, even if he wasn't anything special in bed. He had to be nearly forty, so what could she expect? He'd probably memorized his moves twenty-five years ago and saw no reason to change them now.

Feck paid her to clean and cook, deliver and pick up an assortment of packages, pretend to be various people, have sex with him about twice a week, answer his phone, make bank deposits, place bets at the track, place phone calls using her knack for accents, and take care of his fish although she could hardly count that chore because she'd killed them within a week. His mother, her next charge, fared better.

Mrs. Feck had one of those diseases—Doe couldn't remember the name—where she could hardly lift her head. So for her last six months, Doe did everything—wiped her ass, fed her oatmeal and scrambled eggs, even held a tissue to her nose, and changed her Depends. She learned how to inject insulin and bathe her without soaking the sheets. She even—and this was the worst of it—inserted suppositories. As a rule, the two of them watched television about sixteen hours a day. The old woman couldn't speak in more than grunts so figuring out what she wanted—and it was mostly about shows on TV—was frustrating. She'd been particularly incensed when the network cancelled her favorite soap.

"Work out a system," Feck told her when she complained. "Maybe she can tap things out like with Morse Code. Or blink yes and no with her eyes." For his part, he saw his mother as seldom as possible. "She wasn't exactly any mother-of-the-year," he said. "I was never sure she could tell my brother and me apart."

"Are you twins?"

"No."

When Doe tried to set up a "system" one time by duct taping a pencil to Mrs. Feck's palsied hand, the old woman shook it off, nearly hitting Doe in the eye. Despite these minor issues, she grew fond of the old lady. Having someone dependent turned her on. Not sexually, but maybe like she was Mrs. Feck's mother in some sense. She wasn't clear on the reason for it.

"I think I might want to have a baby some day," she told Feck after his mother passed. "Or maybe a puppy."

"Good luck with that," he told her. "As long as you're not thinking I'll be the Daddy."

Actually, she'd already ruled out Feck as father material. But he paid her a better salary than she made at the Weekday Café or Tudge's Pub, so as employer material, he'd do. Once in a while, she caught the whiff of something bad going down, an event that gave her pause. One too many Serbian or Bosnian girls turned up on their porch last spring, for instance. And there was the time she heard a man screaming with pain on Feck's cell.

The thing Doe did most often in her new life was wait. Wait for a phone call, for a car to show up, for the bank to open, for the food at a drive-in, in line at the post office, for Feck to call her, for him to finish up in bed. Wait. She'd become very good at waiting.

She had no idea what was in the cards for today. Feck said he'd call her at two and fill her in. Looking at her watch, she saw it wasn't even noon. The next marker on her map was to:

Look for a big-ass sign saying Todd's Cabins.

She found it a minute or two later. A *Closed for the Season* sign hung out in front. There'd be skiing up here in a month, but Todd's was not the sort of place skiers stayed. She doubted even hunters would find their way here. Todd's Cabins probably closed for the season right after Labor

Day—as soon as old Todd needed heat to keep warm, as soon as he cleared his winter's beer money

There were eleven cabins—a number that made her nervous until she realized that one was Todd's office so it didn't count. Odd numbered things always seemed like a jinx. She looked for Number Four. Four was the only one whose windows weren't boarded. She put the key in the lock and pushed the sticking door open.

Whew—something had died in here. But, other than the smell, it wasn't a bad place—two tiny bedrooms and a main room with a kitchenette at one end. A bathroom that was reasonably clean. Todd or Mrs. Todd had made the place kind of homey with plaid slipcovers and curtains, a lacy tablecloth—although it turned out to be plastic—a couple of prints of the northern woods. She could picture spending a week here with the kids in the summer. Kids—that thought kept returning. Had her parents ever stopped fighting long enough to take her sister and her to a place like this? She couldn't remember a single vacation. Bible school was the furthest she'd got from home. The ladies that ran the Bible School knew they were babysitting Sheila and Delores too and made them memorize bible verses while the other kids got to color Joseph's coat.

A dead mouse was in the bathroom and another in the bottom drawer of the stove. Using fireplace tongs, she threw both outside. Several dead wasps lay curled up on the windowsills, but other than that, it was really okay. Smelled like mildew, suntan lotion, insect repellent, and burnt onions once the odor of death was removed. There was some fresh food in the cabinets, more in the fridge. A space heater in each room, which she immediately fired up. Maybe enough stuff for a long weekend. It'd better be because she hadn't passed a store for miles—maybe not since Gaylord. Even the house with the Caddy was four or five miles back.

Cabin Four was the furthest from the road. Feck told her to park her car in the back of the cabins even though there was no road there. Obviously, he didn't want anyone spotting her car and nosing around. What was she doing here anyway? What did he have in mind? It couldn't just be a drug pick-up. Someone must be coming up here for a few days, and she was going to stay too because Feck had made her pack a bag. She hoped she wasn't expected to sleep with whoever it was. Probably not, or Feck would've had her pack differently.

"Just some jeans, T-shirts, and underwear," Feck said. "You won't be goin' out on the town." He looked at her face and said in a wheedling tone, "Nothing's open 'round there anyway."

"What *will* I be doing?"

He hated it when she asked him things like that—preferring not to let her in on the details unless he had to, and only then when it was unavoidable.

A good example—she hadn't known she'd be caring for Mrs. Feck until the night before.

"Her nurse took off," Feck had said. "Do me a favor and stay with her till I can find another minder." Ha!

"Just wait for my call," he'd said this morning. "Things are a little fluid." Still in bed, he'd run a nervous hand through the hair on his chest. "Better get going, honey."

So she did—used to doing whatever she was told by then.

There was a small TV in the cabin, but no cable. She was only able to tune in one channel, so she watched *Family Feud* and some dopey talk show. Hungry then, she heated up some tomato soup using half water and half milk, ate some crackers, and made a pot of coffee.

Two o'clock came and went. She found a Robert Parker book on a shelf in a bedroom closet and began to read. She'd become more of a reader now that she cooled her heels so often.

At three-thirty, she heard a car pull up and ran to the bedroom window. It wasn't Feck's Tahoe but a non-descript Dodge. It sat there for a few minutes, and then a man she'd never seen before got out, opened the rear door, and lifted out a sleeping kid. The boy was maybe about eight or ten, she decided, as the man tossed him over his shoulder like a sack of flour. Had this guy rented one of the other cabins? The man was younger than Feck, maybe thirty or so, and big. He was bearded, but it was neatly trimmed. He wore a hunter's getup with big black boots.

She figured he might be here for deer season, but then he headed straight for Cabin Four, and kicked the door open. Why hadn't she locked the damned thing—up here all alone? She had a feeling that a lock wouldn't have stopped him for more than a second or two anyway. Inside, he looked even bigger.

"You in here?" he whispered. "Doe, right?" When she didn't answer, he added, "Feck said you'd be here."

She walked out of the bedroom. "What's this all about? Feck send you?"

"He never filled you in, did he? Damn limey." He walked into the second bedroom and placed the kid on the bed.

"That kid isn't dead, is he?" Doe asked, her voice shaking.

"Of course, he's not dead. Boy, Feck *really* did keep you in the dark. Kid's our little honeypot, and we're going to take real good care of him." He looked at her. "Or you are anyway. Feck said you were like a nurse."

She stared at him. "I'm not a nurse. What's your name anyway?"

He shook his head. "I'm just here to drop off the kid along with some stuff he'll need. You don't need to know my name for that." He headed for the door. "I'll get the rest of it."

"I can't take care of him. What's wrong with him anyway?" The kid still hadn't moved.

The guy turned around and shook his head. "Damn, Feck didn't tell you squat. Kid's knocked out, and you'll have to keep him that way for a day or two. Till his parents pay up."

A funnel of cold air swept from her throat to her stomach. "What do you mean—keep him that way."

"Keep him unconscious, you know. Just you wait till I get the rest of it." The man trudged back to the car, opened the trunk, and removed an attaché case along with the kind of box paper comes in. She watched, trying to decide quickly what this all meant. Trying to get a jump on things. Her brain was dead though. Terror did that.

"Okay," he said, returning, "the box has some stuff you might need—kid's clothes mostly—in case he pisses his pants, I guess. But the attaché has the important thing." He opened it and took out what looked like a medical kit. "This kit has about a half-dozen or so prepared shots in it." He counted them slowly and aloud. "Eight of 'em."

"What ..."

"You know syringes—I guess." He glanced at her. "Hypodermics. Whatever you 'em. You should know bein' a nurse and all."

"I am not a nurse," she almost shouted, but then lowered her voice. "I am ... nothing."

He shrugged. "Well, whatever you are, you gotta give him one of these injections about every six hours." He paused dramatically. "'Cause if you don't, the kid's gonna wake up and then where will we be."

"You mean he's kidnapped, don't you?"

"Well, duh! Think I brought him here to go to the water park."

She was speechless.

"Feck sent a mask along." He opened the paper box and removed it. It was rubber or latex and looked like Snow White's face. "If the kid wakes up for some reason, you should put this on. So he can't ID you later." When she didn't say anything, he continued. "He's old enough to be able to do it too." He looked her over closely. "You look kinda ordinary to me. But you never know."

"Whose kid is he?"

"Some fat cat works at GM, I think. Feck didn't tell me much. We're at the bottom of the food chain—you and me."

"Not even a name," she asked. "The kid's name, I mean."

The guy let out an exaggerated sigh. "Look, you don't want to be talking to the kid, Doe Re Mi. Get it. You want him out cold until his Daddy pays up. Don't be thinking you're gonna have cocktails with him or something." He looked at the eight syringes in the kit, putting a hesitant finger on one. "You know how to do this right?"

"I guess." What was the point in denying it?

She was trying to understand why Feck thought she'd be up for such a thing. Nothing she'd done could touch this. All right, she'd show him. She'd be out of this cabin as soon as the hairy joker left. She could be in Canada in a couple of hours. Or did you need a passport for that now? Damn 9/11.

He must've sensed her line of thought. "You know he's got all kinds of stuff on you, right? Keeps a file on all of us. If you think ole Ruthie's living the life out in Vegas, you don't understand Feck at all."

For a minute, she couldn't think who Ruthie was. "What do you mean—a file?"

The man reached into his pocket and removed a small envelope, handing it to her. "Said to give it to you if need be." Inside was a photo of her exchanging money for drugs in a park in Detroit. Another showed her removing the license plate on a Camry out in Warren, the GM Tech Center right behind her. Bent over, her ass looked as big as a basketball. Why had no one told her this? She swallowed hard.

"Feck's been setting you up for bigger stuff ever since you turned up. Testing you in little ways. But don't worry about this little escapade." He nodded toward the bedroom where the boy was. "This one's gonna go off like clockwork." He paused, looking at her carefully. "Kid gets his next injection at 7 p.m. Then one every six hours after that. You gonna remember that? Know how to set the alarm on your phone?"

"What if something goes wrong?"

"Nothin's gonna go wrong, worrywart. Just wear your mask if he starts to come 'round—wear it when you give him his meds too. Don't be a hero. If he yells, no one can hear him out here. But keep him asleep. A doctor fixed it all up. He'll be fine. This doc fixes tranqs for dogs on plane trips all the time—big dogs even. This is the same deal."

"Tranqs for dogs," she repeatedly numbly.

On his way out the door, he grabbed her car keys from the table.

"Hey," she started to say.

"Don't worry. You'll get 'em back when I pick up the kid." He shrugged. "Look, you could bolt, but we can't have him here all by himself. Don't want him to wander into the woods and get eaten by a bear. You got your phone, right?"

"Right."

Who could she call—that was the first thing she thought. She was in this—whatever it was—up to her neck. Her second thought was did she bring her charger? The third was who would she call anyway? Feck cut her off from everyone long ago. Not that there'd ever been a big social scene in her life.

"Oh, and one more thing. Feck might call you to take a picture of the kid. Know how to do that? Take a picture and send it to him?"

She nodded.

"Practice by taking one of me now."

What world did this bozo think she lived in? Dully, she pulled out her phone and complied.

"Now send it to me. Just for practice." He gave her his cell number and in seconds, he had the photo.

"Good. Wow, I could use a haircut," he said, looking it over. "Now I'll take your picture." He made her pose with the kid on the bed, making her put a hand on the boy's cheek, hold his hand. Nurse Doe.

She did all of this numbly, not taking it in right away. Not figuring it out.

After that, he erased his number from her phone and took off. "Doesn't matter, of course, It'll be in the trash five minutes after Feck has it. Guy doesn't miss a trick."

For the next three hours, she sat staring at the kid, thinking about how dead she'd be if anything went wrong, leaning over him every few minutes to be sure he was breathing. She hunted on Safari for missing kids. Nothing. She plugged her phone into the charger then and crept around the house, looking for something though she'd no idea what. She gave the kid his next injection and continued to watch him, only leaving the bedside to pour some cereal. She could've guessed Feck would choose Fruit Loops. The milk tasted like cream. She finished the coffee from earlier.

She needed to stay awake, but around ten, she fell asleep anyway, waking to find the boy staring into her face. It looked like he wasn't fully awake. She realized after a second or two, he couldn't really see her clearly between affect of the drugs and the dark of the under-lit cabin. She considered putting on her mask just in case, but his eyes were fuzzy and unfocused. It was too early for his next injection so she kept still, and gradually his eyes shut and he fell deeply asleep again.

Where the fuck was Feck? She dialed his number and left a message. "Call me, you jerk." She began reading her Parker book again, remembering the ending sixty pages in.

The kid started coughing about six a.m., a few hours after his next injection. His forehead was hot, really hot. Shit. Would it be safe to inject him if he was sick? She called Feck again. Still no answer, so she left a detailed message, trying hard not to sound too angry, too dangerous to him.

Another hour passed. She found some aspirin in her purse, and after grinding a tablet to a paste, held a finger to the kid's lips. Perhaps intuitively, he licked her finger. It was probably just a simple cold, but she began to worry more. She put on her mask and woke him up.

He didn't seem surprised to see a woman in a Snow White mask. Perhaps his life was filled with events like this one. Hers had been.

"What happened to Obama?" he asked sleepily. "Where'd Obama go?

She wasn't sure what he meant until she realized the guy who dropped him off probably wore a mask too.

"Back to D.C. I guess. How do you feel?" She put a hand on his forehead. "You're burning up."

But he was already sleeping again, his breath more ragged than before, his face glowing red. Now she wondered if it was the virus rather than the drugs knocking him out.

She yanked her phone out of the charger, noticing that its power read less than five percent. The outlet must be disabled. If she called 911 for help, they'd have a record of her cell phone number. She knew by now that there was no way this was going to end well: she could end up with

Ruthie—probably in the ground—or she could end up in a cell. But she would not be responsible for letting this kid die.

"There's a sick kid here," she told the woman who answered her call. "Sorry, I'm not sure of his name. Yeah, I know it's strange." She gave her location and the woman knew the spot right away.

"Todd's sure. Just stay where you are," the dispatcher told her. "It'll be a little wait. Our funds were slashed and we have to use the EMS from Petoskey. We'll do our best. Hang on tight."

She knew the woman would not be so conciliatory once she found out what was going on out at Todd's, but it was nice to hear a friendly voice now. After she hung up, she gave some brief thought to fleeing, to even holing up in that caddy. But snow was beginning to fall and it was miles away. Since she had nowhere else to go, she dampened a cloth and put it on the kid's head. She listened to his pulse. She covered him with a warmer blanket. She ground another aspirin. She tried to be his nurse.

And she waited. She was good at waiting.

†

GUNPOINT

Fred Blosser

"At no place in the United States is a lower value placed upon human life than in Fayette County, West Virginia."

—*Cincinnati Enquirer*, May 15, 1904.

This is a story they still tell in the mines and hollows of West Virginia—about two enforcers for hire in the coal camps of the early 1900s, a dealer in spirits from New York named Torrio, two Hatfield boys, two Pinks, and the day they all met at gunpoint ....

There wasn't really a depot as such in the coal camp of Boomer, only a covered siding where the K&M trains stopped. Usually, it was a locomotive drawing a line of boxcars, filled with Italian immigrants who had shipped over to the States to find work in the mines in this year of 1915. This afternoon, under a cold, gray sky with drifting snow flurries, a passenger train from Montgomery stopped and two men got off. One was tall, dressed in black, with a hard-jawed face, steely eyes, and mustache. The other was shorter, with a tobacco-stained beard and clothes that looked like a ragpicker's throwaways.

Each man had a gun in a shoulder rig under his coat. The man in black, Jace Russell, carried a .45 automatic, U.S.

Army issue, and the bearded man, Danville Fuller, wore a German-made Mauser automatic.

A third man stepped forward from the shadow of the overhang to meet them. "Russell? Fuller? My name is Torrio, John Torrio," he said, not bothering to hold out his hand to shake. He had a heavy accent.

It didn't bother Russell that the other man didn't want to shake hands. He didn't like to shake hands either. When he shook hands, it put him at a disadvantage if he had to pull a gun fast.

"I had a hard-a time reaching you by telegram," Torrio said amiably. He was a small man who stood no taller than Russell's shoulder. "I tried in Bisbee, they said you'd shipped out to Manila under contract to the Army to flush out some die-hard Moro guerillas in the Philippines. I wired there, they said you'd returned to the States. Where'd the wire finally-a reach you? Cripple Creek?"

"Hell's Half Acre in Fort Worth," Russell said. "Now, suppose we talk about today instead of last week. You wired to say you'd hire us for five grand for a job here in the armpit of nowhere."

"I'm from-a New York," Torrio said, "where I do business in what you might-a call the medicinal spirits trade, but I got business connections a lot of places, like here in West Virginia, for instance. Me and my partners bankroll a fella name Gerone over in Harewood, who sells beer to the Dago miners here in Boomer. Few weeks ago, Gerone had trouble with a couple of boys who own a saloon down the track there. They said they'd shoot him down like a dog next time he came to Boomer, because this is their territory."

"They have a valid argument on that score?" Russell asked.

Torrio spat. "*Bastardos*! My territory is where I say it is."

"Would those boys happen to be named Hatfield?" Jace asked. "I'd heard that Troy and Elias, old Devil Anse's sons, had bought a joint here."

"That's-a them. Ah, here comes my man Gerone now ..." Torrio pointed to a sad-faced Italian who was approaching the platform on a wagon drawn by two mules. Barrels were packed on the bed of the wagon. "We're going up on the hollow to the Dago camp to sell a little beer. We expect the Hatfields to try to stop us. Five grand to you and Fuller to make sure they don't succeed."

"Are the Hatfields by themselves?" Russell asked.

"I hear that a couple-a Pinkerton men are in town, sworn in as county deputies by the coal owners to keep peace, but they're also making some spare money on the Hatfield payroll. I expect they'll be with the Hatfield boys."

"You know their names?" Russell asked.

"No. Does it matter?"

"Not really. Just curious. I know some Pinks."

"Also," Torrio added, "there's a Black Hand fella from Pittsburgh named Marko Dante, who don't mind if he gets paid by Americans or Dagos. That make a difference?"

"Only that our fee goes up to six grand if we have to do some extra shooting," Jace said.

"Fair enough. Let's-a go then."

Geone clucked his mules along the path that led from the tracks on the wide river bottom up to Boomer Hollow, a cleft in the hills that followed the course of a narrow creek. The siding and the idling train receded into the distance and finally disappeared behind a bend in the creek. At the far end of the hollow stood a cluster of small, frame-built company houses.

There was another gust of cold wind, a scattering of snow. The hills that enveloped the hollow were gray and bleak. Men saw the wagon coming, and hung back nervously as they noticed Russell, Fuller, and Torrio in tow.

"Where to first?" Fuller wondered.

"A fella named Vagliozo is a steady customer who always takes up a collection from his buddies for a big order, so let's go to his place first," Torrio suggested.

Gerone tugged the reins to head the mules in that direction. Vagliozo's was a small shack like the others, its clapboard exterior weathered. Jace saw a man sitting on the porch silently in a chair, leaning over with his head tilted loosely to one side as if napping. Jace looked at Danville. Danville nodded. Each man unrigged his gun.

When they reached the house, Gerone stopped the mule, and Torrio walked over to the man in the chair. "Vagliozo? Hey, *paisano*?" He touched the man on the shoulder. The man tumbled out of the chair. Russell saw that he had a bullet hole between his eyes.

There was a crash of breaking glass from a window, and a rifle muzzle poked out and spat fire. Gerone, hit, gave a cry and fell off the wagon. He tried to get up. Another bullet struck him and tore out the back of his head. The mules shied, alarmed by the gunfire and the sudden smell of blood.

Russell fired into the window, one blast after another, the .45 bucking in his fist. Going in fast before the gunman in the house could fire again, he hit the door with his shoulder, burst it open, rolled inside. Fuller, watching from the wagon, heard more gunfire. A moment later, a lanky man in a suit walked out through the doorway, a Krag rifle dangling loose in one hand. There was a puzzled expression in his eyes as he looked down and saw the mess that three .45 slugs had made of his chest. His legs collapsed and he went down.

Fuller hurried around the house as the back door flew open and another man ran out. The man saw him, turned, fired a .38—too wildly—and the shot missed Danville by several inches. Fuller's return shots didn't miss. They hammered the man back pitilessly, and as he wobbled on his feet and tried to raise the .38 again, Fuller fired two more times. The man went down.

"That's-a Troy," Torrio said, joining Fuller. "And the other guy, that was Elias."

A shot whipped across the yard, so close that Danville felt the wind in passing. He dropped to one knee, pivoted, and emptied his magazine. The shots took out a dark-complexioned Calabrian who had been hiding on the other end of the house.

"Must be Marko Dante ... guess that finishes it," Fuller said, putting a plug of Bull Durham in his mouth and biting off a chaw.

"Not quite," a voice said.

Fuller and Torrio whirled around. Two men wearing deputies' badges on their coats stood there with guns out. They had approached unobserved during the gunplay. One was a wiry, weathered, mustached gent with a Stetson, somewhere in his fifties. The other was a considerably younger man, not much over twenty, tall and thin, with a shock of russet-colored hair.

"You must-a be the Pinks," Torrio said.

"Yeah," the older man said in a Texas drawl, surprising to hear in the hills of West Virginia. "My name's Charlie Siringo, and this here young fella is named Sam—Sam Hammett from Baltimore, new to the agency, but he's got a steady trigger finger."

"Charlie," Jace Russell's voice lashed out from the house, "whether it's steady or not, your young pal's trigger finger isn't worth a flying fuck right now—you should have been more careful. I've got the drop on you. Put those irons down, you two."

Siringo glanced at the dark window, where only the muzzle of Jace's gun was visible, and dropped his own pistol as his buddy followed suit. "Oh hell, Jace, I heard you'd bought in with Gerone's bunch. I thought Elias must have iced you in the house. I should have known better. Where'd we see each other last? On Joe LeFors' posse, chasing Kid Curry after the Parachute Train Heist?"

"No, I think it was over Fancy Gap way, tracking down Sidna Allen after the Carroll County Courthouse Massacre. You with the Pinks, me with Baldwin-Felts." Russell ambled into Fuller's line of sight, .45 raised.

Siringo's face was imperturbable. "You going to cut us down, too? I don't suppose I can appeal to old friendships?"

"Hey, Torrio, dealing with Dante put our fee up to six grand," Fuller cackled. "Seven if we off these two guys with the tin badges."

"You want to put in a bid and top that, Charlie?" Jace asked, eyes icy above a frosty smile. "Say, eight grand?"

"Hell, Jace," Siringo said, "we're just a couple of hired men, not the royal fucking Hapsburgs. I doubt that

Pinkerton's would go eight bits for us, especially after the shitty job we did today."

"Looks like your call, Torrio."

Torrio shrugged. "I dunno, fellas, I can go-a six for Dante, but I don't-a have seven for these-a two."

"Well, then," Russell said, "I guess it's your lucky day, Charlie. This is business with us: no cause to use our smoke wagons unless we're paid for it. You and the youngster there, Hamlet or whatever his name is—you load Gerone's body on the wagon, then scat. Leave those guns there, though. I don't want bullets flying around us when we go back down to the tracks to catch the last express to Charleston ..."

†

Fair Warning

Hilary Davidson

The letter arrived in a plain white business envelope with no return address. Inside was a page that read, *Stay away from my husband, you bitch. Or your life is over.*

Emily stared at it in disbelief. Was it a practical joke? The letter didn't feel like a prank. She turned over the envelope. On the front was a white computer-printed sticker that read *Emily Eldridge, Senior Editor, Bridal Beauty Magazine*, with her office address on East 46th Street. In the upper-right-hand corner was a canceled Forever stamp with an image of Johnny Cash on it. There was nothing indicating the sender's name.

She got to her feet so she could peer over her cubicle wall. "Vanessa?" she called. "You've got to see this."

"What?" Vanessa half-spun in her chair, turning to face her. Her auburn hair bounced over her shoulders as if she were in a shampoo commercial.

Emily passed her the strange missive. Vanessa pulled out the letter, read it with a frown, then stuffed it back inside the envelope. "Where did you get this?"

"It was in today's mail."

"Are you dating a married man?"

"Of course not!" The words were out of Emily's mouth before she considered her answer. Was it possible Jason was married? She'd only known him for a few weeks. He'd spent nights at her apartment, but she'd never visited his. What if he wasn't single after all?

"Have you ever gotten a letter like that before?"

Emily shook her head. "No."

Vanessa pursed her lacquered lips. "You haven't lived in New York long enough to know, but there are some really sick creeps around. People you'd never expect."

"That's supposed to make me feel better?"

"It's not my job to make you feel better." Vanessa handed her the letter. "It's my job to give you fair warning. To put you on guard, if need be."

"Why would I need to be on guard?"

"Ask whoever you're involved with."

That left Emily deeply unsettled. When she returned to her sublet apartment on Jane Street that evening, she searched for threatening letters in her mailbox, but only found a bill and a J.Crew catalog. She considered texting a question to Jason but decided to play it cool. When she saw him on Thursday night, she lost all reserve.

"I got a weird letter at work," Emily announced, before they'd even taken their seats at the café. "It claimed I was messing around with someone's husband."

Jason's eyebrows shot up. "Seriously?"

"What I want to know is, are *you* married?"

Jason stared at her. "You think I've got a wife hidden away somewhere?"

"I have to ask."

"Yeah, I've got a madwoman in the attic. I can't let her out because she'll try to kill me and burn everything down."

Normally, she found his literary references charming, but this wasn't a normal night. "You'd make a lousy Mr. Rochester."

"Well, it's not me. Maybe it's some other guy you're seeing."

It was on the tip of Emily's tongue to answer that she *wasn't* seeing anyone else, but that sounded desperate. She and Jason were hanging out, not boyfriend-girlfriend. It was clear to her that he was seeing other people. The last thing she wanted was to appear like a clinging vine, so she let the matter drop.

A week went by, and Emily almost forgot about the letter. Then, early one afternoon, she opened a cardboard box and found a large brown rat inside. She screamed before she realized it was dead. There was no note.

Vanessa's head popped over the cubicle wall. She shrieked, too.

Barbara, the editor in chief of the magazine, clipped over in her four-inch Louboutin reptile-skin heels. She was a perfectly preserved blonde in her mid-forties who wore Prada suits and carried Hermès bags. Half the month, she was out of the office, jetting to honeymoon resorts for breathless feature stories that she penned with dizzying regularity, or for corporate retreats with company management. "What's going on?" she demanded.

"The box ... I just ..." Emily stammered.

"Someone sent her a rat," Vanessa said.

Barbara looked inside the box, contemplated the contents, and shut the lid. She didn't scream. Her eyes narrowed. "Why?"

"Why?" Emily parroted, confused.

"Why would anyone send you a dead rat?"

"I have no idea."

"I don't like trouble," Barbara said. "Don't bring your personal problems to this office, is that clear?"

"But I didn't ..."

"Vanessa, make a note of this, please." Barbara's voice was icy. "For the personnel file."

Emily couldn't believe the editor-in-chief's reaction. "But I haven't done anything wrong!"

"Bringing a disaster like this to the magazine's doorstep is doing something wrong," Barbara said. "I certainly hope I never hear about this again."

"You won't," Vanessa promised. "This won't be like the situation with the intern."

The temperature in the room dropped suddenly. Emily could almost see the air frosting over between the two women.

"We don't want to attract the wrong kind of attention around here." Barbara frowned at Vanessa. "I expect you to manage any issues that come up. You *are* the managing editor, after all. Can I trust you to do that?"

"Yes, Barbara."

"Very well." The editor-in-chief turned on her stiletto heels and clipped back to her office.

"What happened with the intern?" Emily asked.

"Never mind that. Look, you don't want to get on Barbara's bad side," Vanessa whispered. "She's allergic to any hint of scandal or negative press. She'd fire you in a heartbeat if she thought you'd make her look bad."

"But someone's threatening me," Emily said. "I should report that."

"Right, go talk to the NYPD," Vanessa said. "That will get you far."

Emily felt her stomach sink, but she had to acknowledge Vanessa's point. No one had been hurt. The police weren't going to waste time on a dead rat in a box.

She felt sheepish telling Jason about it. "Seriously, a rat?" he asked. "It sounds like you're dealing with some kind of jealous bunny boiler."

"It's kind of scary," Emily admitted.

"Has anything come to your apartment?"

"No boxed rats or threats, if that's what you mean. Just the office."

"That's interesting. Whoever is doing this knows your name and where you work, but not where you live."

Emily hadn't thought of it that way. It *was* far easier to track her down at work than at home. She'd only lived in New York for three months, and in that time, she'd sublet two apartments. It made the strange situation more curious.

As the days went by, the shock of the rat receded. But there was a new, unwelcome surprise. Emily discovered emails with sexually suggestive subject lines creeping into her email box on a Friday morning; by the afternoon, it was a full-fledged tidal wave of smut. *Filthy Tramp* were the words that came up most often, but there were all kinds of phrases that seemed more appropriate for a bathroom wall.

"Vanessa?" Emily called. No answer. Emily stood and looked over the cubicle wall. Vanessa's computer was on and her coat was hanging on the edge of the cube, but she wasn't there. Distraught, Emily sank into her chair. She couldn't talk to Barbara. The editor-in-chief's cold blue eyes would probably melt if she saw Emily's screen. In desperation, Emily called the IT department. "S'up, dawg?" drawled a bored voice.

"Is that Bryan?" Emily asked, remembering the bald, tattooed guy who'd set up her computer when she started with *Bridal Beauty*.

"Yep. What do you need?"

"My email account has been taken over by spam. It's pouring in right now." Emily glanced at the screen. Since she'd picked up the phone, another dozen scummy messages had piled in.

"Let me take a look," Bryan said. Emily heard some furious tapping. "Did you post your email address on Craigslist with an ad calling yourself a sexy slut?"

"Of course not!"

"Well, *somebody* did." More tapping. "I'm reporting it. Craigslist will pull it down. And I'm shutting down your account."

"But I need email access," Emily pointed out. "I have a bunch of people to get back to before the end of the day."

"I'll set up a temporary account for you. What's your middle name?"

"Simone. Why?"

"That's going to be your temporary ID. Simone at Bridal Beauty Mag dot com. Pretty name," he added, before reverting to business mode. "Okay, log out and log in again with your usual password."

"I don't know if I remember it."

"That's because you stay logged in all the time, which isn't smart," Bryan cautioned. "It's Currer underscore Bell."

"Right." Emily was just a little embarrassed. "Thanks for your help."

"You want some free advice?" Bryan asked.

"What?"

"Break up with that guy. He's not worth the trouble."

Emily flushed bright red. Obviously Bryan had read her emails to Jason. Humiliated—even though she knew what she sent from her work account wasn't explicit—she sent Jason a text from her phone. *We need to talk.*

She opened her mail while she waited for Jason to reply. That was when she found a white envelope without a return address. Inside, on a plain sheet of white paper, was typed: *I gave you fair warning. Prepare to suffer, bitch.*

Emily staggered to her feet. Vanessa still wasn't back, so there was no one around to talk her out of what she needed to do. She grabbed her coat and took the elevator down.

She didn't know where Jason lived, but she knew the graphic-design firm where he worked. It was only a half-dozen blocks from her own office, and as she walked down Madison, she wondered why they'd never met up in Midtown. That question was answered when she got to his office.

"I'm sorry, but Jason had to run out," the receptionist told Emily. She was an earnest girl with big brown eyes. "I didn't realize he had an appointment on his calendar this afternoon. I would've called you."

"Is everything okay?"

"His son fell at the playground and hit his head. The kid was apparently up and bopping around afterwards, but they wanted to be safe and check him out at the hospital."

Emily's mouth was dry. "His son?"

"Nathan. He's almost two."

"Thank you." Emily blinked rapidly, pretending her eyes weren't filling with tears.

She made her way back to her office, still gasping for air. Vanessa was in her cubicle with a Cheshire cat grin on her face. But when she glanced up at Emily, she frowned. "Is something wrong?"

"I figured out who's been sending me nasty messages."

Vanessa's brow furrowed. "Really?"

"Jason's wife or girlfriend or whatever she is. The mother of his child."

"That's the guy you've been seeing?" Vanessa suddenly seemed confused. "You never mentioned him having a kid."

"I didn't know he had a kid until this afternoon."

"It's terrible to keep something like that from you. What a creep."

Emily's phone buzzed. It was a text from Jason: *Sorry, rough day. Talk tomorrow?*

She glared at it, before typing, *How's your son?*

There was an pause that seemed to stretch into forever. *Doc says he's fine. Just a bump on the head.*

A tiny part of Emily's brain had been hoping the receptionist was wrong, that she was a new hire who'd confused Jason with someone else.

We should talk, Jason wrote a minute later. *Want to get together tomorrow?*

No. Don't bother me again, she texted back. She turned off her phone.

"Was that the creep?" Vanessa asked.

Emily nodded. Her heart felt heavy. She thought she knew Jason, because of their shared love of *Jane Eyre* and

Almodóvar films and a thousand other common likes that didn't mean much in the cold light of day.

"Let's go for cocktails tonight," Vanessa suggested. "You look like you could use a drink or two."

Emily didn't feel like it, but as the clock passed five, she found herself following Vanessa out of the office and into a bar across the street.

"Men in New York are generally creeps," Vanessa told her as the server brought them two glasses of shiraz. "You really can't trust them."

"I feel like such a moron," Emily admitted.

"Don't blame yourself. It's not your fault."

"Has this ever happened to you?" Emily asked.

"I've met my share of deceptive people." Vanessa's mouth curved into a hint of a smile. "You need to keep your eyes on the prize."

"What does that even mean?"

"Every man wants something from you. You should figure out what *you* want from *them*."

"That sounds horrible."

"It's practical. Mostly, it helps keep you out of messes like the one you're in." Vanessa frowned. "If I were you, I'd be thinking about my next job."

Emily almost choked. "But I just landed here!"

"Well, I'm worried that you won't survive certain rites of passage." Vanessa's gaze drifted over Emily's shoulder, and her mouth opened in obvious delight. "Well look who's here," she said.

Emily turned to look over her shoulder. "Who?"

"That's Seth Thorson."

"Who?" Emily repeated.

"Head of the magazine division. Married to the daughter of the company's founder." Vanessa raised her hand in a little wave. Seth saw her and smiled, making a beeline for their table. He was in his early fifties, with graying hair at his temples. His bespoke suit cost four or five times what Emily took home in a month.

"Vanessa, it's good to see you." Seth Thorson took her hand, holding it as if he were about to kiss it. He turned his wolfish eyes on Emily. "Well, hello, Emily Eldridge."

Emily was stunned that he knew her name. Before she could ask how, Vanessa spoke up. "Would you like to join us?"

"Don't mind if I do." Seth smiled at Vanessa, but he sat next to Emily. "We haven't met, but I noticed you just after you were hired."

"You notice all the pretty hires, don't you?" Vanessa said.

"Of course. That's part of my job, isn't it?"

His warm body brushed against Emily's casually, and he touched her arm deliberately. The attention made Emily uncomfortable, especially when she noticed the wedding ring on Seth's hand.

"So, your wife's in the magazine business?" Emily asked.

"My wife?" Seth looked as if she had just dumped cold water on his fine suit. "No. She ... she does her own thing." He stood. "I should be getting home." He threw a couple of large bills on the table and took off without another word.

"The first rule of Bridal Beauty club is don't mention the wife," Vanessa hissed. "The wife is c-r-a-z-y."

"What?"

"If you're a woman and you want to get ahead at this company, there are two ways. Seth Thorson is the first one." Vanessa downed the rest of her wine. "He has a varied and extensive office harem. But he doesn't pursue women. He expects them to pursue him."

"Are you involved with him?"

Vanessa's laugh was bitter. "Don't be ridiculous. The second way, my dear Emily, is to be indispensible."

"I don't understand you."

"Right now, you're not following either path. Get it?"

Vanessa walked out, her expression sour. Emily didn't understand what was wrong with people. Why couldn't they be honest? That thought trailed after her as she left the bar and kept her company all weekend. It made her ignore the texts that came in from Jason. She wondered if she'd made a mistake moving to New York. From her perspective, the Big Apple was crawling with worms.

On Monday, when the mail-room guy came around, she noted with relief that there was no mysterious letter for her. Still, her happiness was short-lived.

Claire, the intern, came over to Vanessa's desk after lunch. "There's a letter for somebody named Simone," Claire said.

"Simone who?" Vanessa asked.

"There's no last name. Just Simone at *Bridal Beauty Magazine*."

"That's odd. I've worked here for three years and I've never heard that name," Vanessa said.

Emily stared at her screen. Simone was her middle name. But nobody knew that. No one except Bryan the IT guy.

"What should I do with it?" Claire asked. "I know you told me to forward all the mail for Laura Childs to you, but what about ..."

"Shhh!" Vanessa made an impatient hissing sound. "Give it to me and go away."

Claire moved off, grumbling. Emily heard Vanessa slide a letter opener through the envelope. "What was that about?" Emily asked, popping her head over the cubicle wall.

"Hmm? Oh, nothing. Just some junk mail about a line of wedding dresses."

Emily bided her time until Vanessa got up from her desk. Then she circled around the cubicle, feeling uneasy. The envelope addressed to Simone, no last name, was in Vanessa's recycling bin. Inside, was a typed note: *Steer clear of my husband, you bitch. I'm not going to warn you twice*.

Emily folded it back into its envelope and headed for the stairs. She walked down two flights, finding her way to the den of iniquity that belonged to the tech guys. She headed straight for Bryan and handed him the envelope. "What *is* this?" she asked.

He took the note out, read it, and returned it. "Looks like someone doesn't like you stepping out with her husband."

"Take a look at who it's addressed to," Emily instructed him.

Bryan did a double-take. "Your temporary account?"

"You set that up on Friday. Some crazy person mailed me this letter on Saturday, and it just arrived."

"Who did you email from the account?"

"Why does that matter?"

Bryan brought up her email account on one of his three screens. "Okay, on Friday afternoon, you emailed a couple of freelancers, the art director, the social-media people, and Seth Thorson."

"That's ridiculous. I just met him on Friday evening. I've never emailed him."

"Well, read it and weep," Bryan said.

Emily stared at his screen. *Can't wait to see you tonight, baby. Our usual spot? I may bring a fig leaf along.*

"You sent it at three-fifteen, immediately erased it from your Sent folder and permanently deleted it from your Trash."

"But ... I was out of the office then."

Bryan studied her. "You were? What about these other times?"

Suddenly, Emily was staring at a screen of mash notes sent from her account to Seth Thorson's. Her heart started to pound.

"I never sent any of these," she breathed.

"Well, somebody did. And if it wasn't you, it was someone who wants it to look like you're having an affair."

"Who would do that?" she said,

"I don't know, but you don't want to end up like Laura Childs," Bryan said.

"Who?"

"She was an intern who had an affair with Seth Thorson." Bryan lowered his voice. "I'm not saying she was the only one sleeping with him. But she got caught."

"What happened to her?"

"She was waiting for the subway one night, and someone pushed her right in front of a train." He shook his head. "From what I heard, they never caught the psycho who did it."

"That's horrible." Emily swallowed hard and sank into the chair beside him.

"You're not going to believe this, but someone's writing an email from your account right now."

"I've got to go," Emily breathed, dashing for the stairs. When she got to her floor, she hurried to her cubicle, but no one was there.

"Doing a hundred-yard dash?" Vanessa asked, from the other side of the wall.

"Did you see ..." Emily was about to ask her, *Did you see anyone at my desk?* when she realized what a fool she'd been. Vanessa had been setting her up all along. She was the one sending messages from Emily's computer, trying to frame her for an affair she wasn't having. What was the game, exactly? Hide her own affair with Seth Thorson by tossing a false trail of breadcrumbs to his crazy wife?

Emily took a deep breath. "Did you know Laura Childs?"

"She worked here for a little while. Why?"

"I heard she was murdered."

"Some lunatic shoved her onto the subway tracks." Vanessa sighed. "She's a cautionary tale around here. You've got to be careful in New York."

A cautionary tale? Emily considered Vanessa's cold phrasing. She'd learned exactly what she needed to know.

After Vanessa left for the day, Emily slunk into her cubicle. Vanessa may have been clever about using Emily's account, but she was clueless enough to stay logged into her own. Emily composed an email to Seth: *I miss you! You promised to come over to my place. When am I going to see you? I know you're just teasing those other girls who email you. I can't wait to be with you again.* For good measure, she added Vanessa's home address, and attached a photo of Vanessa, a headshot that appeared in the magazine next to her etiquette column.

Emily anxiety rose as she left the office. She didn't know whether Seth Thorson's furious loon of a wife would take the bait. Deep down, she was terrified that the woman was lying in wait for her in the bowels of the subway station. Panicked, she took a taxi home. The next day, she called in sick after a long, sleepless night. She kept the television off, stayed away from email, and lost herself re-reading *Jane Eyre*.

The next day, she returned to the office, feeling more than a little sheepish. But that feeling only lasted until she saw, Claire, whose eyes were puffy and red.

"Is everything okay?" Emily asked her.

Claire took a shuddering breath. "Vanessa's dead. She was stabbed outside her building yesterday. I still can't believe it. The guy who did it didn't even take her bag."

Emily hid in her cubicle that day, afraid to have any contact with anyone. She was broken by guilt and the knowledge that Vanessa didn't deserve to die. But she hardened her heart with resentment. Vanessa had been setting her up to die, after all. Maybe Vanessa had set up Laura Childs, too. She told herself that she hadn't had a choice, and she believed it.

The rest of that week was quiet. There was a well-attended funeral and a brief flurry of tabloid coverage. Then Barbara, the editor-in-chief, called Emily in for a meeting. "I need someone I can trust to be managing editor. For all intents and purposes, you'll be running the magazine. Can you handle that?"

"Yes," Emily promised. "I can do it."

She hired a new editor, Wendy, to take her old job. Barbara was away at the time, so it was a couple of weeks later when Emily was called into the editor-in-chief's office again. "I don't like that new girl," Barbara announced. "She seems like so much window dressing."

"She's smart and a very hard worker," Emily countered. Why was Barbara threatened by Wendy's looks? The new hire was stunning, but also friendly and outgoing.

"People are talking about her. I don't like that." Barbara crossed her arms. "But I supposed we'll try her out for a bit."

The meeting left Emily unsettled, but Barbara didn't bring the subject up again. Emily forgot about it until a few weeks later, when she heard an exclamation from Wendy's side of the cubicle wall. She stood and looked over. Wendy was staring at a white piece of paper.

"What is it?" Emily asked.

"*Stay away from my husband or I'll end your life before you can blink, you bitch,*" Wendy read. "Is this supposed to be some kind of joke?"

"No," Emily whispered, feeling her world falling out from under her feet. "It's no joke."

†

THE FOLLOW-THROUGH

Chris F. Holm

You know your problem, Matty? You got no goddamn follow-through.

Matthew Graham was drunk. That fact wasn't much of a surprise. Matthew Graham was often drunk these days—used to be, he worked construction, but ain't much call to hire an unskilled high-school dropout when the market was flush with trained craftsmen just itching for work—and anyways, drunk was the only time he ever thought about his father. Matt's pop was a florid, hirsute, meaty guy with a scraggly horseshoe of dark brown hair draped around his pate from ear to ear, and an unkempt lawn of scruff to match. He had a big mouth, big hands, and a big appetite for the coffee brandy, the latter of which often summoned the former, at least until he drank enough it summoned sleep. And every rant, every ass-whupping, always started the same way.

You know your problem, Matty? You got no goddamn follow-through.

The bitch of it was, Matt thought as he peered skip-visioned from drink at his shithole of a third-floor Lewiston walkup from his perch on one threadbare end of his scratchy, thrift-store couch, his old man had a point. A hundred-odd cases of beer aside, Matt had never finished a thing in his life. Most of the time, it didn't bother him none. He was content to coast through his days wherever they took him—even if that was just from bed to couch and back. He was a man of few wants, and consequently of few worries.

At least, until he met Kylie.

Then, all the sudden, Matt knew from want and worry.

Kylie lived across the hall, a pretty sad-eyed waif with a laugh as fleeting as it was magnificent. Matt fell for her the first moment he laid eyes on her—sleep-addled and pajamaed in the dead of night, her eyes glistening with tears, her hair a haphazard bun atop her head as she stood outside smoking on the stoop—and sometimes, he half-thought she felt the same. But he never made a move, because she'd been shacking up with a string of deadbeats since long before they'd met, each leaning heavier toward the beating side of the equation than the last. Matt thought that it was Oxy that kept her seeking out these bums, but it seemed to him a vicious cycle—he was pretty sure she started popping pills to dull the ache of morning bruises, and then endured a whole new round come evening to ensure they'd stay long enough for her to score some more pills. Most of her suitors didn't stick around longer than a week or two—growing bored, maybe, or moving on to goods less damaged.

Until Dana, that is.

Dana Arsenault was some twenty years Kylie's senior—a scruffy big-boned guy with a dodgy comb-over and flashpaper temper, who, truth be told, reminded Matt of his old man. Guy'd been on disability for years—some kind of accident at the textile mill where he used to work the looms—which meant an endless, meager string of checks on which to live, and an endless supply of pain meds to kill the pain and boredom both. Where and how Kylie'd hooked up with him, Matt didn't know. But why she stayed with him despite the nightly screaming matches Matt heard through the walls—which invariably led to the sounds of muffled blows and muffled cries—wasn't hard to guess.

"Honestly, I don't know why you put up with that douche," Matt told Kylie one day while they lounged smoking on the building's stoop. "You could do a whole lot better."

"All you know is what you hear," she told him, her eyes opiate-glassy and unfocused.

"Ain't that enough?"

Kylie shrugged. "Dana isn't always that way."

"Yeah, sometimes he's asleep."

At that, she laughed a little, and placed her hand atop Matt's. "It's sweet you worry about me, Matty. Makes me feel safer knowing you're around."

Her touch made his heart soar. Her words did their best to break it. Because he knew deep down they were so much bullshit—every night, while Dana was going at her, Matt just doubled down on beers and turned his TV up until he could half-convince himself there was nothing going on at all.

Guess his old man was right about him.

Least, until that night.

It started the same as always. A slamming door. Their voices raised. Matt grabbed another can from the fridge and drank it two-thirds down before he got back to the couch. Then he sat down heavily and waited for the slap.

Instead, the building shuddered, and he heard a sound like a sack of potatoes being slammed against a wall. Then the sack of potatoes wailed in pain and fright, and before

Matt knew what was happening, he was fumbling drunkenly at the lockbox he kept beneath his bed—the one that held his birth certificate, his Social Security card, and his grandpa's rag-wrapped gun. A stubby little .38 his granddad used to use to scare off crows, it hadn't been fired since long before the old coot died. But the machine-shop scent of gun-oil still clung to it, and the rounds he thumbed into its chambers with rage-shaky hands slid in easy enough.

He was across the hall in seconds, pounding on Kylie's door. Matt's pulse thundered in his ears, Kylie's cries filling the silences between. Why Dana opened the door, Matt didn't know. But it was the last mistake he'd ever make.

Matt didn't expect the gun to be so loud. A sonic boom inside the tiny space, the gun struggling against his grip like a creature frightened by the sudden noise, while in front of him the hairy boxer-clad piece of shit—Dana, Matt reminded himself, not his asshole pop—pirouetted, gouting red. It was disgusting and hilarious and wrong and oh so right.

Matt heard a commotion behind him. Looked back out through the open door to see his neighbors fleeing down the hall—some in panic, some with cell-phones pressed to ears. He eyed them with confusion for a moment, as if from a great distance, and wondered idly what all the fuss was about. Then tiny fists battered his chest and brought him back to the here-and-now.

Kylie. Her bruised face twisted into a mask of fury. Her sad eyes no longer sad but full of hate.

"You stupid son of a bitch! What the fuck were you thinking?"

"I ..." Matt said. "He ..." but nothing else would come.

"Why couldn't you leave well enough alone? You just killed the only guy who ever gave a shit about me—and for what? Now the cops're gonna come and take his stash—not to mention *your* dumb ass—and *then* what the fuck am I gonna do?"

Matt looked at Kylie, suddenly a sullen junkie in his eyes. Looked at the scruffy dead man who so resembled his old man, lying in a pool of spreading blood on Kylie's floor. Heard the rising cry of sirens fast approaching.

You know your problem, Matty? You got no goddamn follow-through.

Oh, yeah, old man? Matt thought. We'll see about that.

Then he closed the door to Kylie's apartment, and shot twice more.

†

GRANNY PANTIES

Sophie Littlefield

The thing she hung onto, in the end, was the granny panties.

Who can say why? It wasn't like she set out to keep a souvenir from that other time, that dark time when eighty extra pounds served as a daily reminder that she was nothing and would never be anything. That she was dirt clinging to the sole of a shoe—the world's shoe, a world indifferent to her pain and shame and longing.

In time she had a whole drawer full of pretty new things, satin bras from Victoria's Secret, Hanky Panky thongs at eighteen bucks a pop from Nordstrom. Thongs! Who would have believed it possible? Not her. Not Frank, certainly; Frank who went down on her with a zeal that almost frightened her—Frank who had never and would never see a picture of her from before.

Yet at the back of the drawer, crumpled unlovingly, was a pair of white cotton panties, size XXL. They were nearly new, unstained, barely worn, and from time to time she would spot that flash of pure white among the black and lacy bits she wore now, and the thought that went through her head, if she registered a thought at all, was—Thank you, God.

There were worse things in the world than gratitude. Certainly there were worse habits than prayer.

But it wasn't God's name she invoked the day she came home to find the idiot great-nephew of the woman in 1B, the drug-addled waste of humanity whose own parents kicked him out of their home after one late-night summons to the police station too many—to find this pale and fragile acne-crusted boy going through her drawers looking for something, anything he could sell—to find him holding the hated things in the air, regarding them with adolescent amusement that turned to fear as he stared across the gulf of the panties at her fury.

God was not on her mind when she got the gun from the hall console table—she'd protested but Frank was the first man to ever want to protect her, a notion she couldn't be expected to resist—and leveled it at the boy with a steady hand.

And "Do it now or I'll fucking kill you" could never be mistaken for a prayer, but the boy—as he pulled the granny panties on over his grimy jeans, his skinny hips, and stood regarding her in mute horror—worked his lips in a way that suggested he was chanting something holy. The Apostles' Creed, perhaps, though he made no sound and didn't look like a boy who'd been forced to go to church.

†

There You Are

Keith Rawson

"No matter where you go, there you are."

I was five the first time I heard her say that. Five years old and I was upset and crying because we moved from the Montana mobile home park we'd been living at for nearly three months. I was crying because the park had been full of kids my age, and we played all summer and talked about starting kindergarten in the fall. I really want to go to school with my friends.

She'd spout this shit into my ear for the next eleven years of my life and move us fourteen times. Fourteen different states during that time: Montana, Wyoming, Washington, Massachusetts, Vermont, Maine, Florida, Louisiana, Texas, Nevada, New Mexico, Colorado, California, and finally we circled the drain in Arizona.

Obviously the woman didn't believe a single fucking word of her mantra.

By the time we ended up in Arizona, she finally got tired of the road and left me in a Buckeye motel room, and I never saw her again.

Gone.

Gone and me sitting watching HBO, in the air conditioning, two nights paid up.

Eight hours after she was gone, I knew she wasn't coming back, so I headed to the front desk of the motel with my fake ID that said I was 22 and asked the frazzled looking guy behind the counter if he had any work.

The frazzled-looking dude behind the counter was named Ed Laurie. He owned the motel, and his son had quit two months earlier to go live with his boyfriend in San Francisco, and Ed had yet to find anyone who was willing to work graveyard for $6.15 an hour. Ed hadn't slept longer than three hours a night in two months, and when I asked for a job, he pulled out an application, had me fill it out, and hired me on the spot as long as I started training with him right then and there. He was so desperate, he didn't even notice that I had listed my address as his motel.

Ed was a good dude, I ended up working for him for ten years until someone shot him when he was covering for me on my day off.

* * *

My buddy Andy came by at 10:00. Andy used to work at the Amazon warehouse, but he got fired for stealing books. Dude worked in a warehouse full of HDTVs and Blu-Ray players and he got busted for lifting 2000 copies of some shitty James Patterson thriller; he thought he could drive them all to Phoenix and sell them at a couple of used bookstores down in the valley. Like most everything, Andy didn't know dick about what people read. It pissed me off when he got fired, I was hoping he could get me in during Christmas. I never let him know I was pissed because he still came by with news of day labor and the occasional quarter bag he didn't want to sniff up on his own.

Andy was pale, not that he wasn't always. Lived his whole life in the middle of the hottest desert in America and the dude looked like a ghost. But this time, he was the kind of pale you get right before you're getting ready to puke. I thought I even noticed something dried and yellow on the side of his mouth, so maybe he'd already done his puking and was starting to feel better.

"What the fuck's wrong with you?"

He took his time answering, rubbing his hands together, his jaw clenching, unclenching trying to get some kind of noise past his lips.

"I got a little work tonight."

It was ten o'clock at night, fucking late for me. I'm an early riser, always have been. It used to drive me nuts when I worked graveyard because just as I was wanting to go to bed, my body was wanting me to get up, stretch and maybe go for a jog. I started in on the pills for that shit. But I hadn't worked graveyard in a couple of years, so I just let myself fall asleep when I was tired and wake up when my body wanted to wake up.

"It's late, dude."

"I know, I know." The fuck he did, he'd probably had just gotten up a couple of hours ago. "But I need the help. It's good money, man. Fifteen hundred bucks, but it needs to be done now. It can't wait until you wake up."

Fifteen hundred bucks would pay the rent on the trailer for three months. Three months without having to worry about a roof over my head was nice. Maybe I could try stretching it out, pay only two months, and then work day jobs only when I needed to. Shit, who am I kidding. I'd probably just do what I always did—get fucked up, but do it for a couple of weeks instead of three or four days.

"Alright, what are we doing?"

"Come on, it's out in the car."

Andy didn't have no fucking car. I mean, he did when he worked at Amazon, but his mom took it away when he got fired.

He was driving a pimp wagon: pitch-black Beemer with twenty-inch rims, orange neon strapped to the undercarriage and those euro headlights that blind you when you pass them on the highway. I'd seen the ride around town and ain't never seen Andy behind the wheel of it. A lump popped up in my throat when he waved me over to see the dead nigger in the trunk.

* * *

The woman who raised me wasn't my mother. My mother, as far as I know, lived in Philadelphia with my father. The woman who raised me said her name was Glenda Spelling. She said she used to be a nurse; she said she was the nurse who helped my mother squeeze me out. Glenda said when she saw my mom and dad, both of them sixteen and black, she knew they were fucked. They were fucked because they were teenagers, fucked because they were black, fucked because they were probably drug addicts, or drunks, or my dad beat up on my mom or he would start after a few weeks of dealing with a crying baby in the middle of the night and not getting any sleep at all.

But because of all these things Glenda made up in her head when she saw my parents, she figured I would be fucked too if I stayed with them. The way Glenda saw it, no baby deserved to be so screwed. She thought babies deserved a chance for a decent life and she thought she could give it to me because she was a pretty white lady with red hair and people always treated her nice. So when she saw my parents come through the emergency room doors, she knew she had to save me.

The delivery was short. Glenda said she laid me on my mother's chest, and then helped my father cut the umbilical cord, and then she walked me out of the room and then out the hospital doors. She told me all of this when I was five when she told me to stop calling her mommy and start calling her Glenda. A couple of months before she left me at Ed's motel, she changed her story and told me she took me because she was tired of being a nurse and she figured she could get more welfare money if she had a kid. She said she couldn't have one of her own because her plumbing was no good, so she decided to just take one.

Glenda was all kinds of fucked up.

* * *

"You can't smoke in here, man. You've got to put that shit out."

The car belonged to a seventeen-year-old kid named Trim. Trim's real name was Carl and his Dad works at the prison. There's this little group of kids in Buckeye, all of their dads and moms work at the prison either as guards or food service workers, or whatever. The group have all been friends since they were little kids; all of them growing up listening to stories from their parents about prison gang wars and riots; the whole thug-life thing. The kids think the stories all sound cool as hell and they start acting like the guys in the stories to piss off their parents; the usual teenage rebellion bullshit. The kids take the shit too far—make a little gang, deal dope, b&e's, hold-ups; trying hard as fuck to get into the place where all their folks worked.

The king dick was Trim. Trim didn't give a fuck. Trim didn't give a fuck because he had all the drugs; if you're a shitheel little kid or a low-rung scumbag like Andy and you want to get high, you have to go to Trim. I've only met him a couple of times and wanted to kick his teeth down his throat both times. He's one of those guys who thinks if you're black you need to act like a movie gangster, and if you don't, he thinks you're weak. I always thought that shit was stupid; I'm 6'4, 250, and darker than Wesley Snipes. So in a place like Buckeye, I already stick out like a black tooth, and I take enough shit from the Sheriff as is, but if I was wearing jeans hanging off my ass and fat gold chains, I imagine they would have a holding cell named after me at a couple of the Maricopa substations.

Trim didn't fuck with me too much because of my size, but I wanted nothing to do with the little nigger other than to score.

The problem with country motherfuckers like Trim is they think they're hard and are always looking to prove it. With Trim, the dude was always talking shit about killing off the other little wannabes who cut into his action. There weren't all that many, only a couple of kids who bought off his guys and the Mexicans. You didn't fuck with Mexicans, they have their own thing going on, and if you get mixed up in it, you ain't long for this world. That left the kids who bought off of him to fuck with when he got bored. It was nothing ever too rough, a little ass kicking, a drive by where all the bullets were shot up in the air.

The body in the trunk was Trim finally going too far.

He was some kid from the middle school, maybe thirteen or fourteen. From what Andy told me, all the kid was doing was selling pot that he was getting off his cousin in Phoenix instead of distributing the dirt-brown shit Trim was known for pushing. Andy said the kid was mouthing off a little bit. Said he was puffing out his chest, trying to out movie-gangster Trim, that's when Trim pulled out his gun and shot the kid through the throat.

"He started fucking crying, man. Balling his eyes out, telling the kid to stop fucking around and get up."

Trim watched the kid bleed out in the dirt, crying, and finally realizing that playing with guns and actually using one are two completely different things.

It was just Andy, Trim, and the kid, none of Trim's boys, just the three of them. Trim begged Andy to help him, begged him to help get rid of the body. By the time they got it loaded up into the trunk, Trim lost his nerve, said to Andy he couldn't help him. Told him he would give Andy whatever money he had on him, just as long as he never had to see the body again. Ended up that whatever money Trim had on him was three thousand bucks.

"He tried to bitch, but then I told him it was a small price to pay for peace of mind."

"And not having to touch a dead kid again."

"Yup."

But then Andy started getting wiggy. Started thinking about digging a hole alone out in the middle of the desert; thinking about the cops pulling him over in Trim's car if

Trim decided to be a bitch and call it in stolen. So he came to my place because I know how to calm him down, keep him center. Plus, he knew I wouldn't turn down fifteen hundred bucks.

"Where are we gonna put him?" Andy asks, the orange and green of the dashboard lights making him look like something rotten.

"Let's take him out where we put Ed," I said.

* * *

Ed was a good man, but he was a coward, spent his whole life jumping out of his skin at the sight of his shadow. It's no way to live, but it was just who he was.

I had a lot of fun with him over the years. I'd jump out at him from behind the Coke machine, crank calling him from one of the unoccupied rooms until he finally stomped down to the room and I would come at him from out of the closet wearing a Freddy Kruger mask, laughing my ass off while watching the front of his pants going damp.

It became hobby.

That's why I didn't think he would pull a gun. I thought he would throw up his hands when Andy walked in wearing panty hose over his face and waving around a .22 demanding all the money in the register. All I thought Ed would do was shit himself, maybe puke.

Nope.

See, Ed might've been a coward, but the one thing he would lay his life on the line for was money. Ed worked hard. He did all the maintenance around the motel, all the cleaning, worked the front desk, everything. He took pride in the place even though most of the people who stayed were usually the type of people you wouldn't piss on if they were on fire. But it was Ed's: no mortgage, no debt. Every dime went in his pocket, and he'd rather die than let a single cent find its way into the wallet of anyone who didn't earn it.

You can't really blame Andy or Ed for what went down. It's natural. You see someone getting ready to harm you, you react. Andy just happened to be younger and faster and a really surefire shot.

After we buried Ed in the desert, I waited a few days before I called the cops to report him missing. I told them Ed had gone into Phoenix and had never come back. I could tell the cops wanted to pin it on me—I mean, that's just how it works, right? Blame the black kid. Even though Ed would take me out to dinner every Friday night, even though he treated me like his own flesh. Even after they found Ed's car in some shithole neighborhood in Mesa, I could tell that the Sheriff still wanted to charge me. But in the end, they had shit on me or Andy, I made sure of that.

I thought after Ed's estate was all settled that his kids would still want to keep the motel up and running, maybe make me manager. But neither one of them wanted a thing to do with it. They had their lives out in California, and that was that.

I was out on my ass, and the only thing I had to show for five years of my life was the six hundred bucks Andy grabbed after he shot Ed.

* * *

Digging a hole in the desert is hard. Most people when they think of the desert, they've got this picture in their heads of loose dunes of orange and yellow sand. Arizona desert ain't nothing like that. The ground is orange clay, dense, full of rocks and tangled roots. Dig deep enough and you're sure to run into veins of copper, crumbling shale, and black volcanic rock so hard that you might break a shoulder trying to muscle past it.

When Andy's shovel clanged and set off sparks down in the hole, I thought it was some of that volcanic rock.

"Fuck!"

We'd been digging for two hours. I started the hole, shucking four feet of dirt over my shoulder. I wasn't going any deeper, I have a fear of tight spaces, so there was no way I was going in the ground, $1500 or not. So in the hole Andy went, huffing and puffing with each shovel full, bitching under his breath until the blade struck stone.

"What is it?"

"I don't know? Shine the light down here."

I threw some light on him and see what his shovel hit.

Rib cage.

Shredded lime-green shirt, black mold growing on the patches.

Grinning skull, clumps of faded red hair still clinging to the scalp.

"Holyfuckingshit!" Andy scrambled out of the dirt, leaving the shovel and a puddle of piss.

Glenda.

It's funny how the mind remembers things, you know. For years now, my mind's been telling me that Glenda walked away, leaving me to live with Ed. Of course, I've been trying to bury most things Glenda; her eyes when she'd get bugshit mad, the way she smelled after a week of no sleep and rocking meth with the bikers she liked hanging out with, the way she treated me.

A good mind, a solid mind will protect itself. It will protect itself from the beatings, the days without food or water, of me breaking Glenda's neck, of me driving out in the middle of nowhere and putting her in the ground, then driving back to our room and falling asleep with the TV on like I didn't have a care in the world.

And I'm sure, eventually, my strong mind will block out Ed getting shot, my life in Buckeye after Glenda, or of me putting a pickax through Andy's head, of me burying him and the little shit Trim killed together, their arms entwined like two napping toddlers.

Of course, the three grand in my pocket and my brand new BMW will help my memory some. I'm sure with that kind cash and this kind of ride, I can be whoever the fuck I want to be no matter where I go, at least for a little while.

†

The Blow Jobs

Josh Stallings

The strike of your fist on your face carries a weight like no other. Believe me. Or check it out. Just don't pull the punch. Don't pussy out at the last moment. The second one? Hurts no less. Neither does the hammer.

They say at moments of extreme pain, one twin can feel what the other is going through. I hope that isn't true.

* * *

We grew up in Glendale, came of age in the golden dawn of glitter rock. Had Dad lived to see me and Caleb in our skintight jeans and feather boas, he would have whupped our asses. Then again, if he'd survived past our seventh birthday, we might have chosen a more macho form of expression. Fuck that, I'll put Bowie up against any band going. What were we supposed to rock out to? Boston? Rush? Fuck that noise.

What I remember most about Dad was he always dressed like a cowboy, wore a white straw hat, Western-style belt. Bought the belt at a lawn sale. When he was drinking he'd tell women that he won the belt riding bulls back in Texas. Trouble was, there were only three bars on Brand Blvd. So odds were he had either already told them the story or it was them he bought the belt off of. I wonder if he ever nailed any of those women. Wonder if he ever had a fumbled fuck in the men's room. Or was faithful to Mom. She was a worn-out woman. Gray. Yeah, that's the word, she was gray. It was almost like she wasn't there even when she was sitting across the table from me.

It was a chaotic violent home. Any infraction up to and including playing cartoons too loud when Dad had a hangover won you a dance with the belt. Caleb and I look so much alike, sometimes even Moms, as we called her, couldn't tell us apart. Dad would yell at me, "Seth, get your candy ass over here. You cry, I'll do it even harder." Caleb would hop up, take the belt without even flinching. "Good little man, Seth," Dad would say, "good little man." Then he'd kiss the top of Caleb's head. Tenderness only came on the tail end of pain. To be clear, I never asked Caleb to take my whippings. Never. I also never asked him not to.

* * *

I hang my head, finding the strength for the next self-inflicted blow. I'm wearing work gloves. I have a roll of quarters gripped in my palm. This punch lands on my brow, hard enough to open it. Blood rolls over my left eye. In the background there's a slight pop in Bowie as ground control does its final checks. Before putting it on, I had wiped the record with a black velvet cloth and blew the dust off of the needle. It should be pop-free. Caleb and me stole the Technics turntable from the booth of some teen disco in the Valley. The kids running the joint were in the back getting high on the shitty pot we sold them. The turntable was just begging us to heist it.

As I'm sitting on the kitchen floor, blood is dripping off my chin. It is hitting the linoleum to the beat of Bowie's countdown.

* * *

Six hours earlier, I got the call. "Seth, you got to, fuck, you know, fuck?" It was Lenny.

"Dude, slow. Where are you calling from?" He was supposed to be out on a party boat in the San Pedro bay with my brother. A gambling scam they set up.

"Caleb has fucked up for the last, final, never-fucking-again time."

"What does he owe?" I ask.

"Never mind .... Six grand. But that is far, far from the fucking point."

* * *

Caleb and me met Lenny in seventh grade, became thick as thieves, and not just because we were the only Jews in our grade. We bonded over Bowie. Lenny had his long hair hennaed carrot orange. We went full glitter, not a look favored by the Armenians and Mexicans at Glendale High. Apina, hot pants to her crack, giant of a girl, hot-hot-hot Apina, was our fourth Musketeer. At fifteen, we four learned to shoot dope together. Learned to creep houses. We were a rolling petty crime spree.

Lenny, Apina and me, we all got clean the summer before our twelfth grade. We still drank and smoked Marlboros like chimneys, but no dope. My brother never did get clean, or more like he did and then didn't and then did. His addictions roamed from smack to speed to whiskey to strange pussy (this last one almost got his Johnson taken off by Apina), to pot, but always back to smack, all other addictions orbited the mighty opiate. Gambling with money he didn't have was his latest rush. When sober Caleb was an amazing guy. Those six or seven days a month were almost worth the twenty-three of pure bullshit.

I was the opposite. I hated risk, pain, loss. I had a big secret kept from all these motherfuckers, Caleb included. I loved books. Loved them. When I was five, Dad caught me reading *James and the Giant Peach*, thought I stole it. Caleb took that belt for me. But he laughed his ass off at me that night, "*James and the Giant Peach*, what kinda lame ass crap is that?"

At school I hid my reading, so I wouldn't get moved from Caleb's class. Only the librarian knew I was reading three or more years above my grade. Caleb and me divided school chores easily, I did homework and he kicked any ass that needed kicking. This deal got more complicated in high school. Caleb would fuck up, steal the football coach's car, I'd return it as Caleb and talk them out of pressing charges, convince them it was a prank.

Caleb wanted to be a rock star, didn't sing or play an instrument, but that didn't hold him back. Apina wanted to be whoever it was she needed to be, to be by his side. Lenny, he wanted to be a gangster: Micky Cohen, Israel "Ice Pick Willie" Alderman—these guys were who he emulated. His uncle was connected to the LA family.

Broke punk in a torn glitter T-shirt, my dream was the wildest. I never said it out loud. I wanted to be a writer. Or failing that a lawyer. I loved words, but, with Caleb for a brother, a lawyer might be more practical.

* * *

"I got two grand, three and a half if I sell the Bonneville," I told Lenny.

"You aren't hearing me, Seth. Money won't square it. I give Uncle Margolas the six, maybe he kills Caleb quick. Bottom line. Real, real bottom line. Caleb is not walking away this time. You been protecting him since junior high, we did, I love him. But this shit is beyond our reach."

"We protected him? Bullshit. He is always there for us."

"Not when he's high."

Lenny was right, and Lenny was full of shit. Even high, Caleb protected our asses just by being himself. Strutting Glendale in our eye make-up and platforms we were the perfect target for the Mexicans, Armenians, hell, any ball player who just got his SAT scores and realized he would die with roofing tar under his finger nails could kick our ass. But they didn't. Lenny was sure we were a bad ass crew. We weren't. Caleb was the reason they cut us a wide berth. By the eleventh grade, he would die before he took any more shit from anyone. The bullies all saw that in his eyes and backed the fuck off.

* * *

Thirty-six hours earlier, Lenny, having seen a high school production of *Guys and Dolls*, put together a floating card game. He thought it was a brilliant plan. But like all brilliant plans cooked up when stoned, it had multiple fatal flaws built into the underpinning.

THE MARKS: Persian college students. The deal with them, and this isn't racist, or maybe it is, what the fuck do I know. They loved to snort coke and fuck teenage tang. They were willing to pay big cash to get to party with the glitter kids. Lenny met them in Hollywood earlier that year. He was scalping tickets to an Eagles show, they were buying. He up-sold them to a cool party after the show. Spent the whole show arranging the cool party. By dawn we were all high as kites and a grand richer. After that night he kept them on the line. Hung a couple times. Reeling them in. Setting the hook for a real score.

THE BACKER: Uncle Margolas was a real deal, feed-you-to-the-fishes gangster. Lenny made a bold move when he convinced Uncle Margolas to bankroll this floating party. He laid out fifteen Gs, two muscle boys to keep it from coming off the rails, and a big-titted dealer who could guarantee the luck ultimately broke our way. Down in San Pedro, Lenny found a party boat with a skipper whose morals shifted with the cash flow. Caleb put together a party pack of upper and downers, muscle relaxers, ludes, poppers, coke, lots of coke. High rollers loved their coke. I pimped as much top-shelf booze as I could. Apina was in charge of filling the boat with willing lovely ladies.

THE PLAN: Get these Persian millionaires looped, and, while they got stoned and laid, we could take them to the cleaners at the card table. The Persians, I call them that like I'm talking about a nation. Reality, they were a group of five, sometimes up to eight, guys. Persian students over here going to USC. They had ass loads of cash. When they graduated they would go home, put on the turbans or whatever, marry the arranged wife, and live a traditional Muslim life: no cigs, no booze, and no teenaged gash. These parties were their last shots at freedom. If losing at cards kept them at the party, they were happy to lose. They were there to get high with American glitter kids and bone hot teenage girls.

* * *

At 9 p.m. sharp-ish, the *S.S. Party Until Your Cash Runs Out* set sail for a three hour tour, a three hour tour. Or however long it took to shake the Persian's pockets clean.

Seven glitter girls lounged around looking alluring, all rabbit fur and ruby lips.

Here was the problem.

The main girl, and by far the hottest, is Apina. She is six feet tall in her platforms. Platinum pixy haircut. Leather mini skirt that just covered her bush, and that tube top everyone hoped gravity would pull down and expose her damn near perfect breasts. It would be creepy for me to think of Apina that way. So I didn't. She was Caleb's girl. Always had been. He was in love with her. At eighteen, love looks and feels real as can be, maybe it is. Fuck do I know.

* * *

I hadn't joined them on the party boat, might have gone very different if I had. Who knows how fate works. Facts were, I was neither good at cards nor tough. And I was prone to puking on boats. So I stayed home. I was filling out financial aid papers. I hadn't told any of them, but I had been accepted into Whittier College's creative writing program. If I didn't cut it as a writer or lawyer, I wanted to teach, anything that didn't end up with me driving a forklift or wearing a paper hat like the rest of the guys around us.

* * *

Thirty minutes into their voyage all was copasetic, money was flying around the table. Caleb was up, then down, then up.

Stop. Back up. Here's a bit of pertinent history, or at least it feels that way to me, and, as the guy bleeding out in a dingy kitchen, what I say goes.

We grew up tough, broke, on the kick your ass if you look at me wrong side of Glendale. Our old man was crushed by a poorly stacked forklift when Caleb and me were seven. After that, our mother cleaned houses and offices, and she worked a night shift at a gas station. Dad had worked union his whole life, so they gave us twenty-five bucks a week. We had to pick up cash from the union hall from Mr. Salvatorio. He gave me the creeps. Always sweating. He insisted one of us boys pick up the cash. Caleb always did it. Said I was a sissy and some punk would take it from me on the walk home.

After Caleb started collecting from Mr. Salvatorio, he changed. He would go someplace in his head. His eyes would be staring at you, but he was looking through you to some horror only he saw. This scared other boys in the neighborhood. Rumors started that he was a stone killer.

As tough as Caleb was, and he was tough, he'd wet the bed. I'd pretend I was sleeping, but even in the dark I could see the tears running down his face while he switched his sheets. We did the laundry, we cooked, we cleaned. Moms worked so many jobs, only time we saw her was when she was sleeping on the sofa. We'd kiss her as we went off to school. Don't know if she felt it.

* * *

I scream and scream when the hammer head hits my left pinky. I hit it again before I lose my nerve. Bowie says, "*May God's love be with you ....*" I crush my thumb. I bite a chunk out of my tongue and my mouth is full of blood. I stain my Nico T-shirt.

* * *

We stopped getting the union money when we turned ten and Mr. Salvatorio got retired with an ice pick. That was the rumor, many hoped it was true. Some said Caleb did it. He didn't, I'm sure, but it helped cement his reputation. From then on Caleb and me, we both worked after school. Or I did. Caleb never told me where his share of the cash came from.

By the time we were sixteen, Moms had "passed," sweet term for dying. Almost like there was something on the other side. Died with a broom in her hand sweeping some other lady's kitchen. I hope she didn't go to the other side with a broom still in her hand. She deserved a rest.

Sixteen meant we would be sent to foster care, and at our age than meant juvie. They said we needed a guardian. So we found one. Mrs. Harris in 2B. It cost us twenty-five a month plus a half hour of her boring stories about when she was the personal assistant to some movie star neither of us had heard of, to get her to say we lived with her. It took some artful scamming, tidy paperwork and dodging home visits, but we were eighteen before they caught on and by then it was too late. No retroactive foster care.

* * *

Sixteen. The year Caleb taught me how to pay the bills for real. We had three main cash makers. Dealing Mexican rag weed in the high school parking lot. Creeping houses (not worth the risk, we should have been taking down houses in rich neighborhoods, but we knew fuck about them, so we robbed people with only slightly more that we had). But the big money, the Murphy, that deal was old school.

We'd go downtown, by the Bonaventure or one of the other big hotels. Apina would entice a businessman in town for a convention or whatever to hire her for a quick bj. She'd lead him into an alley, drop to her knees, and as soon and his pants were down, POP! POP! I'd snap a couple of quick Polaroids, Caleb would rifle the pockets. We'd take cash, watches, sunglasses, credit cards. Never wedding rings. That was Apina's rule.

Caleb made a big point of studying their driver license, letting them know we'd mail the pix if they ratted us out. Sometimes it was a few hundred, others it was huge. Caleb knew a guy in East L.A. who bought all the credit cards we could get. Most days there was enough cash to get high, pay the bills, and take in a show at the Palladium. Glitter-Rock Robin Hoods. That was what Caleb called us.

It got real ugly only once. We were hung up waiting for a cop car to pass. By the time we hit the alley, the John had his cock out and his hands gripping Apina's hair. Caleb laid boots to the guy. Stomped him near to death. There was blood everywhere. Apina was crying. I was crying. Caleb was laughing while he kept kicking the guy. Apina and I finally dragged him away. We called 911 from a pay phone. I hope the guy didn't die. Getting a blow job from a teenager seemed a sad thing to die for.

* * *

I'm glad Mom passed before things came apart. Wasn't her fault. Wasn't Dad's for getting crushed. "Just the luck of the draw," Caleb would say, "sometimes you pull aces and sometimes two's, and sometimes you pull an ace when what you really need is that two to make a straight."

* * *

Back on that fateful fucking party boat. The weather started getting rough. Everyone was coked to the gills. Drinking Champagne and sniffing poppers. The Persians were spending like, well, like drunken Persians. Problem is.

And there is always a problem.

Some girls are eye candy.

Some girls like to fuck these guys.

Sometimes the guys give a girl that likes to fuck a nice piece of jewelry.

Sometimes it's worth a load.

Does this make the girls who fuck the Persians whores?

Fucked if I know.

Point here is, Apina doesn't fuck anyone but Caleb. She is strictly eye candy. Period. End of fucking story.

* * *

I bring the bat down onto my knee. I can't scream. I'm choking on blood. It takes several more hard blows before I get even the slightest of cracks from the knee. *I have lost all contact with ground control. But I think my space ship knows which way to go.*

* * *

On the slow-rolling upper deck, Caleb's luck had gone south. Even with the dealer on his side he was still losing. He was down six Gs, he needed to regroup. If you lose house money in a fixed game, they will fuck you up. Looking for a discreet place to shoot some dope, not get high, just even, he walked downstairs.

He heard a muffled scream.

He kicked in a door.

He found one Persian holding Apina while the other had his dick in her mouth.

Caleb stepped out.

Then Caleb went back in.

He had a fire ax in his hand.

The man holding Apina stopped when the ax severed his head from his spinal cord.

Apina pushed the man humping her mouth away. The man fell on the bed.

Caleb buried the fire ax in his chest. Again and again and again.

The room went silent, only Apina's quiet whimpering and Caleb's labored breathing.

The party upstairs continued. Laughter. Giggling girls. Iggy yelling out. The pop of another cork. No one noticed as two bloody kids slipped out a window and clung to the side. They were off the boat and running before the crew had even tied off. Nothing was thought of their hasty escape until thirty minutes later when the bodies were found.

* * *

That was when Lenny called and explained the monumental cluster fuck we were in. Uncle Margolas and his boys had suddenly found themselves involved with, and had to clean up after, a double homicide.

"I guess it's time I tell Caleb about the rabbits." I said to Lenny on the phone.

"Rabbits? The fuck, Seth, this is real. They know where you live. You got to give him to them. Only play left."

"Rabbits Caleb, and you can feed them ..."

"Seth, come back to earth ... you have no time."

Apina said Caleb never liked to French kiss. Said it made him feel like he was being smothered. Almost what being forced as a kid to blow a union boss must have felt like.

"Seth. Dude. Time is ticking."

Yes it was. "He's my brother. It comes from me. He is my brother." Hung up. Started to ring. I ripped it out of the wall.

* * *

Ten minutes ago, Caleb and Apina came out of the bedroom, showered and changed. "So the pope goes to his cardinal as says ..."

"Caleb, they are coming. For you. Apina?" She shrugged. Caleb is just high enough to function but not real well.

"So the pope, being a curious old fucker, he asks, 'What's a blow job?'" I slapped my brother for the first time in our collective lives.

"You are out of time. Whatever else was happening. It happened. Now you need to roll, big brother."

"Two minutes doesn't make me the big brother, Seth."

"Seems like it did."

"Yeah, guess it did." He looked sad, contrite, like always after he fucked up big.

"Lenny can't hold off his Uncle's boys. You have to go." I can't imagine it, "Now." Gave him the keys to the Bonneville, it was registered in my name so I gave him my license.

"Where, Seth, where? I never once didn't see you every day. Never once."

He is right. This moment is not possible. Thought it would never happen.

Thought we would always be *us*.

Now he had to become *he*.

I was crying like a bitch. Pushing him toward the door. "You got Apina. Head north. Seattle. Head anywhere but never back here."

"Never." His eyes glistened, but I knew he wouldn't cry while I was watching.

I hugged him hard enough to last a lifetime.

I kissed Apina.

I heard them drive away.

I pinned a note to my chest, "This is what is left of my only brother Caleb, kill him if you must. Or leave him be. Walk away. He is done. I'm done too. I will disappear now." I signed Seth for the last time. Live or die, it would be as Caleb.

On the 134 a Peterbilt let out a long air-horn moan.

I thought of all the ways a life can go.

I wished I had gotten to write a book.

I wished I'd had a woman look at me the way Apina looked at Caleb.

I wished my time hadn't run its course so soon.

I took a long breath, letting it out slowly.

Then I went to work.

The strike of your fist on your face carries a weight like no other.

"This is Major Tom to ground control ... I'm stepping through the door."

†

The Speed Date

Kieran Shea

CHARACTERS:

Peter: Late 20s to early 30s, groomed, slightly bookish, precise in movements.

Claire: Mid to late 20s, pretty, vivacious, from Texas.

SETTING:

Present day. A two-top at Mexican restaurant outside of Washington, D.C. A speed dating event.

* * *

PETER *and* CLAIRE *sit across from each other. They have pints of beer and a basket of tortilla chips with a shallow dish of salsa between them.*

PETER: Okay, ready? Cyber Persona Targeting Analyst.

CLAIRE: Get out.

PETER: It's true.

CLAIRE: (*Retracting slightly*) Seriously? That's your job title?

PETER: Yup.

(*A beat*)

CLAIRE: For the CIA?

PETER: It's a bit more complicated than that.

CLAIRE: Oh? Try me.

PETER: Well, it's like this. Langley contracts the work guys like me do to an umbrella group over in Crystal City and that group, in turn, serves as a gatekeeper.

CLAIRE: A gatekeeper?

PETER: You know, like a workflow distributor? They dole out said work to smaller private outfits like the one I work for. There's this huge swath of cooperative intelligence initiatives these days. If you follow the news you've probably heard about it.

CLAIRE: You mean like the NSA thing?

PETER: I'd like to think we're a bit more buttoned up than that, but yeah. See, the overall US intelligence reach, the CIA along with DHS, NSA, the Pentagon and a bunch of the overspill agencies, they're all doing it because of the staggering workload. (PETER *uses his hands to demonstrate*) There's this (*beat*) insane pressure to stay on top of everything. The parameters domestic and global keep changing all the time. Proactive external defense outsourcing it's called, a.k.a. PEDO for short.

CLAIRE: Boy, there are a lot of acronyms in this town.

PETER: (*He holds his beer with two hands, looks down*) True.

CLAIRE: And this place you work for is down in Alexandria?

PETER: Uh-huh. Not Old Town proper, but just southwest of the King Street metro. We're based there, but we go wherever the jobs take us.

CLAIRE: How so?

PETER: Well, for example I just finished up a gig in Palo Alto this past Wednesday, and I've a two-day stint in Miami starting next week. Mostly we get assigned work in the mid-Atlantic corridor though. This is our backyard. The big wigs like to use us to keep their travel costs down.

CLAIRE: What's it called?

PETER: Trust me, you've never heard of it.

CLAIRE: C'mon. D.C. isn't New York. It's practically a small town.
(*Pause*)

PETER: Jupiter Global Strategies.
(*A beat*)

CLAIRE: You're right. I've never heard of it.

PETER: See?

CLAIRE: It was a lot sexier when you said the CIA.

PETER: And easier to explain. (*A whistle blows offstage, right*) Phew, there's that lady again.

CLAIRE: (*Annoyed and looking behind her*) Jesus, what's her deal, huh? She's practically a drill instructor with that thing. I think it means we have five minutes left.

PETER: Not a lot of time.

CLAIRE: (*Turning back*) Guess we better make it count then, huh? So, you must be super smart, I mean, having a job with a fancy title like that.

PETER: Not really.

CLAIRE: Are you being modest?

PETER: I'm more of a geek than anything.

CLAIRE: That wasn't my first impression when you sat down.

PETER: Nice of you to say.

CLAIRE: Where did you go to school?

PETER: Pardon?

CLAIRE: School. You know, college? You probably went to some big engineering school or something, that's what I reckon.

PETER: Actually, I didn't go to school.

CLAIRE: Hold up. You didn't go to school at *all*?

PETER: Not unless you count the military and the US public educational system.

CLAIRE: Wow.

PETER: (*Sighing*) I mean, I suppose I could've gone to college, but with tech stuff these days what's the point, you know? You can practically teach yourself everything you need to know if you have the aptitude and put your mind to it. Discipline is the key.

CLAIRE: How does that even work?

PETER: (*Shrugging*) Well, with hands-on stuff like the stuff I do the big intelligence wonks are more interested in you passing their criteria than anything. I mean, when you think about it, everybody lies nowadays, on their resumes especially. The people I subcontract for? They use us because they want disciplined worker bees that can get the job done without all the ego baggage and there's less risk.

CLAIRE: So, then how did you end up at, wait, where did you say you worked again?

PETER: JGS? Long story. Do you really want to know all this?

CLAIRE: There's plenty of time.

PETER: Not according to Miss Whistle.

CLAIRE: Nutshell it then.

PETER: Well, let's see. After my second tour I heard about JGS from a buddy of mine. I applied on a whim and the next thing I knew I was whirling through a bunch of interviews and then a series of these hardcore tests. Of course, once I passed those hurdles they did a whole boatload of FBI background checks on me to corner up my security clearances and after that there was some off-site training. I was, like, pretty much golden in a few months. To be perfectly honest, I was thrilled they wanted me because they cleared me from enlistment obligation. But enough about me. How about you, huh? What's your deal?

CLAIRE: (*Drinks some of her beer*) My deal is duller than dull.

PETER: (*Checks his watch*) Now, now. Fair is fair and quid pro quo. Where'd you go to school?

CLAIRE: You're the brainy self-starter. Take a wild guess.

PETER: A wild guess, huh? Mmm, okay. Let's see. (*He looks her over appraisingly*) Nice top dollar jeans, ski-tags on your jacket not anywhere on the east coast ... tooled cowboy boots and kind of an outdoorsy vibe overall so I'm going to venture ... Colorado? University thereof?

CLAIRE: No way.

PETER: What?

CLAIRE: Get out. You did not just say that to me.

PETER: What? I was right?

CLAIRE: Hell, yes, you were right. You're totally freaking me out right now. I grew up in Houston and went to U of C Boulder for the skiing ... along the way I got a BS in ecology.

PETER: That's amazing.

CLAIRE: Do you, like, have some kind of telepathic chip in your head that scans my dossier back at *der bunker* in Langley?

PETER: (*Laughs nervously*) You know, I've always liked the sound of that word.

CLAIRE: What word? Langley?

PETER: No, dossier. It's one of those words that is a bit of a mishmash. French obviously, but it also comes from the Latin—dorsum—which means back, like a shark's dorsal fin? The French roots supposedly reference bulging bundles of office papers bound up with straps that had labels affixed to their spines like dorsals. Dossiere also means the ridge of a horse's harness.

(*A beat*)

I do a lot of crossword puzzles.

CLAIRE: But still, out of all the schools in the country you up and pick the University of Colorado? How did you do that?

PETER: Just lucky I guess.

CLAIRE: Right. Sure. Lucky you guess.

PETER: Sheesh, it's not that big of a stretch. Mediums scam people with probability techniques on TV talk shows all the time.

CLAIRE: Is this something they teach you at your job?

PETER: No, but I was way into magic tricks when I was a kid.

CLAIRE: But the odds—

PETER: Odds schmods. What does it matter anyway? I tell you this though. You do have that athletic, outdoorsy charm about you.

CLAIRE: Oh I do, do I?

PETER: Yeah. Very attractive. Honest to God, I was waiting for this whole circus to cycle through and for you to sit down.

CLAIRE: Aww, that's sweet. (*Drinks some more*)

PETER: The other women here tonight at this speed dating thing? I don't know. They all kind of look like in ten years they'll be sitting in traffic in some huge SUV, powering down on a nine dollar iced latte and stuffing their kids full of veggie snacks in biodegradable bags in the backseat, all pissed off and wondering what the hell happened to their lives. Sorry. That's me being kind of a jerk. Or maybe it's D.C. The people around here ... they get to you after a while.

CLAIRE: No, I totally get what you're saying.

PETER: Besides, you're drinking draft micro beer. Let me tell you, that's definitely a plus for a warm-blooded, hetero dude like me.

CLAIRE: You're so funny.

PETER: I try.

CLAIRE: I saw that you rode your bike here earlier.

PETER: Aw, man, you saw me pedal up on my steed outside? Dang.

CLAIRE: So, what's up with that, huh? Do you ride bikes a lot?

PETER: For blowing off steam mostly. I'm not into the whole triathlete scene or anything.

CLAIRE: Don't you own a car?

PETER: Sure, but Friday night traffic in Northern Virginia and D.C.? Riding my bike here seemed a lot quicker.

CLAIRE: Smart thinking.

PETER: Built it myself actually.

CLAIRE: Oooh, a man of many skills.

PETER: Steel frame, TIG welded, and the whole nine yards. It's a fixed gear track bike, no brakes.

CLAIRE: Seems pretty reckless.

PETER: You just need to think ahead.

CLAIRE: Did you come straight from work tonight dressed like that too?

PETER: What, this? I changed my shirt, but they're super casual at the office. Couple of guys in my division? Bunch of gung-ho fitness nuts. They like to spin up the Mount Vernon bike trail at lunch. They keep nagging me to join them, but I always pass. The truth is I was actually going to join them today, but I bailed because I was committed to this tonight so I thought it best to conserve the old sweat reserves. I hope I don't smell too grubby.

CLAIRE: You smell fine. Gosh ... cyber, gung-ho bike geeks working for Big Brother. I have to say, the mind reels.

PETER: We're a special breed.

CLAIRE: Hey, at least you don't have to wear a pantyhose and heels.

PETER: I take it at your job you do?

CLAIRE: Oh, you better believe I do. The dress code at the law firm is like a nightmare straight out of a Brooks Brothers catalog or something.

PETER: I like the cowboy boots and ski jacket ensemble better.

CLAIRE: So do I. My dry cleaning bills are killing me.

PETER: So?

CLAIRE: So? So, what? My job? God, I don't want to talk about that. It's so lame. I hate it. I took a course when I moved out here so now I do paralegal nonsense for a bunch of junior associates who think just because they passed the bar exam and made it through the front door there isn't a hundred pound rock tied around their necks.

PETER: Sounds charming.

CLAIRE: (*Drains the rest of her beer*) Whatever. I mean, the firm does do a little environmental law, but I think they do it for all the wrong reasons. I'd like to get on the other side of the issues, you know? Fight the good fight? Do something socially productive with my degree, but getting a job with a non-laughable salary at a cool non-profit or progressive lobbying group on K Street takes time. My parents? They want me to use their connections back in Houston, but I kind of want to separate myself from all that, you know? Do things on my own.

PETER: Admirable.

CLAIRE: Thanks.

PETER: Not to freak you all out again, but if you're from Houston, I guess your old man works for a big energy company, right?

CLAIRE: That's two for two, psychic dude. A pipeline development outfit. Duh, like that's a total shocker, right? God, if I want to get anywhere I'll likely have to go to graduate school for environmental studies or worse—law school. My father wants me to seriously consider law, but it's no secret he's more than a little bitter these days after my so called 'four-year vacation on the slopes.' He says he has to finish licking the wounds in his wallet first.

PETER: I wouldn't worry about it.

CLAIRE: Easy for you to say.
(*A beat*)

PETER: Um, can I ask you something?

CLAIRE: (*Flirtatious*) Isn't that what these speed dating events are all about?

PETER: Yeah, I guess so. I just want to be sure of something. I mean, you came to this thing alone tonight, right?

CLAIRE: And you're asking me this now because ...?

PETER: Nothing. I was pretty certain you did but I didn't know if you had girl posse backing you up and scoping me out.

CLAIRE: Paranoid much?

PETER: (*Pushing away his beer from which he hasn't had a drop*) These days, people really should be.

CLAIRE: Well, if it puts your mind at ease the answer is no. I'm all alone tonight. Me, myself and I. Frankly, I was sort of embarrassed to schlep my girlfriends along to this sort of thing.

PETER: I guess there could be a stigma.

CLAIRE: To hell with stigmas. So, what? Why not try a new dating angle, am I right?

PETER: Sure, totally.

CLAIRE: I mean, meeting people these days just plain sucks, but I have to say ... this place? Could they've picked something a little less heavy on the neoned cliché? Maybe back off on the corny south of the border polka tunes? Being from Texas, you have to understand I have that accordion crap coming out of my ears. (*A whistle blows offstage right again*) There's that lady again.

PETER: How much time do we have now?

CLAIRE: Third whistle, one minute warning.

PETER: Right. (*Standing*) Well, it was really nice meeting you.

CLAIRE: (*Looking up at him, beaming*) Likewise. So, do you want to exchange information? I think I have a card. It doesn't have my name on it or anything, but they give them out to us at the law firm. (*Starts fishing in her purse for a card*)

PETER: (*Shakes head*) I don't think that's necessary.

CLAIRE: What?

PETER: In person you seem really nice, but I'm sorry.

CLAIRE: Wait a second. In person? What do you mean in person? Did I say something wrong?

PETER: (*Checks his watch again*) No, I'm just sorry it has to be like this for you.

CLAIRE: (*Suddenly slurring*) Be like what? What're you talking about?

PETER: This. The end. You really should've been more careful about what you read at work.

CLAIRE: What? (*She tries to get up, loses balance, sits, sways, blinks, steadies, etc.*)

PETER: And sharing what you read at the law firm online, even in passing, with your friends on social media that's not a smart call at all. Fortunately the national security damage you caused was minimal. I slipped a toxic nerve agent into your drink.

CLAIRE: (*Indecipherable*)

PETER: Relax, it doesn't hurt. The aneurism drugs we employ now, they try to make them soft. (CLAIRE *slumps in her chair, expires*) See? There. What did I tell you? Soft, soft, soft. I bet you didn't even feel a thing.

(Lights fade)

†

ABOUT THE AUTHORS

PATTI ABBOTT's stories have appeared in most of the usual venues. She is the author of the ebooks, *Monkey Justice* and *Home Invasion*. She won a Derringer in 2009 for her flash piece, "My Hero." Forthcoming stories will appear in *Thuglit*, *Needle: A Magazine of Noir*, *Underground Voices* and a forthcoming David Cranmer anthology. She lives outside of Detroit.

FRED BLOSSER is a native of the town in Fayette County, West Virginia, where the story takes place. At one time, Boomer was just as explosive as the story indicates. He came along some years after the gun smoke cleared. About thirty percent of the story is true. What thirty percent, he'll leave readers to determine. He is a longstanding fan of pulp, Howard, Burroughs, Hammett, Lovecraft, *Black Mask*, Gold Medal, and Old West history, among other things. He has a wonderful family, a great day job, and a home in the Virginia suburbs of Washington, D.C.

HILARY DAVIDSON won the 2011 Anthony Award for Best First Novel for *The Damage Done*. That book launched a series that continued with *The Next One to Fall*—set in Peru—and *Evil in All Its Disguises*, about a missing journalist in Acapulco. Hilary's first standalone novel, *Blood Always Tells*, will be published by Forge in April 2014. She's also the author of a short story collection, *The Black Widow Club*. Her first tale for BEAT to a PULP, "Insatiable," won a Spinetingler Award, and her contribution to *BEAT to a*

PULP: Round Two, "A Special Kind of Hell," was a finalist for a Derringer. www.hilarydavidson.com.

CHRIS F. HOLM's short fiction has appeared in such publications as *Ellery Queen's Mystery Magazine*, *Alfred Hitchcock's Mystery Magazine*, and *The Best American Mystery Stories* 2011. His "Collector" novels recast the battle between heaven and hell as Golden Era crime pulp. He lives on the coast of Maine with his wife, crime-fiction reviewer Katrina Niidas Holm. No, she hasn't reviewed his books.

SOPHIE LITTLEFIELD grew up in rural Missouri, the middle child of a professor and an artist. She has been writing stories since childhood. After taking a hiatus to raise a pair of unruly children, she sold her first book in 2008 and has since authored over a dozen novels in several genres. Sophie makes her home in northern California.

ANDREW NETTE is a crime writer, book and film reviewer, and aspiring pulp scholar. He is one of the founders of Crime Factory Publications, a small press specialising in crime fiction. His short fiction has appeared in a number of print and on-line publications. His first novel, *Ghost Money*, was published in 2012. His website is www.pulpcurry.com. He lives in Melbourne, Australia.

KEITH RAWSON is a little-known pulp writer whose short fiction, poetry, essays, reviews, and interviews have been widely published both online and in print. He is the author of the short story collections *The Chaos We Know* and

Laughing at Dead Men (SnubNose Press) and co-editor of the anthology *Crime Factory: The First Shift*. He is also a regular contributor to *Spinetingler Magazine* and *LitReactor*. He lives in Southern Arizona with his wife and daughter.

KIERAN SHEA lives outside of Annapolis, Maryland, and his debut novel *Koko Takes a Holiday* is forthcoming from Titan Books in 2014.

JOSH STALLINGS is author of the critically acclaimed "Moses McGuire" crime books as well as *All the Wild Children*, a noir memoir. He has been, in no particular order, a film editor, taxi driver, criminal, father, husband, club bouncer, a trailer editor, a screen writer, a bad actor, and a good friend. He lives in the city of his birth, Los Angeles, with his wife Erika, two dogs, and a cat. Find out more at http://www.joshstallings.net

OTHER TITLES FROM BEAT TO A PULP

BEAT to a PULP
PO Box 173
Freeville, New York 13068
USA
Email: btapzine@beattoapulp.com
Visit us at www.beattoapulp.com

CPSIA information can be obtained at www.ICGtesting.com
Printed in the USA
LVOW11s2039031215

465229LV00001B/65/P

9 780991 203901